ASHA *and the* SPIRIT BIRD

ASHA *and the* SPIRIT BIRD

Jasbinder Bilan

Chicken House

Scholastic Inc.

Library of Congress Cataloging-in-Publication Data available

ISBN 978-1-338-57105-9

10 9 8 7 6 5 4 3 2 1   20 21 22 23 24

Printed in the U.S.A.   23

First edition, June 2020

Book design by Abby Dening

*This book is dedicated to my family and especially to
my wonderful majee, Chint Kaur Bilan,
who held my hand throughout my childhood
and still stays close.*

GLOSSARY OF
HINDI AND PUNJABI WORDS

BARFI—A sweet treat made with condensed milk. A bit like fudge.

BETAY—Dear (term of endearment for a child).

BINDI—A red decorative mark painted on the forehead between the eyebrows, usually by married women.

BUTA—An ancient floral symbol shaped a little like a teardrop.

CHAI—Spiced sugary tea.

CHAPPAL, CHAPPALA—Simple sandals a bit like flip-flops.

CHUNNI—A long scarf worn by women, usually to match an outfit.

DEEVA, DEEVAY—A small clay pot filled with oil and a wick, similar to a tea light.

DHABBA STALL—A roadside stall selling freshly cooked food.

DHAL—Soup made with lentils.

DHOSA, DHOSAY—A rice-batter pancake cooked on a griddle and stuffed with a spiced potato filling.

DHOTI—A cloth worn by men instead of pants. You wrap the cloth around the waist and the final section is passed through the legs and tucked into the waistband.

DIVALI—The festival of lights celebrated all over India and by Hindus around the world, based on the story of Rama and Sita. Candles are lit, fireworks set off, and presents exchanged. The festival is also part of the Sikh religion, where it celebrates the release of Guru Hargobind from prison.

DIVALI MUBARAK—Happy Divali.

JELAYBIE, JELAYBIA—An orange spiral-shaped sweet treat. It's crunchy on the outside and filled with liquid sugar.

KABADI—A traditional Indian sport, a bit like rugby without the ball.

KHEER—Indian word for rice pudding.

KURTA—A knee-length tunic worn over pants.

LASSI—A drink made with fresh yogurt, water, and ice.

LENGHA—A long, pretty skirt usually worn for special occasions.

MAHOUT—A person who looks after elephants.

NAAN—Soft white-flour flatbread cooked in a tandoor oven.

NAMASTE—"Hello" in Hindi.

PAAN—A red leaf from the betel tree, chewed like tobacco.

PAISA, PAISAY—An Indian currency unit, similar to cents in the United States. One hundred paisay make a rupee.

PAKORA, PAKORAY—A fried potato-and-onion savory snack made with chickpea flour.

PANEER—Soft cheese, often cooked with peppers, onions, and tomatoes.

PARATHA, PARATHAY—Layered whole wheat flatbread filled with potato and smothered in butter.

ROTI, ROTIA—A flatbread made with whole wheat flour and cooked on a griddle, similar to a Mexican tortilla.

RUPEE—The currency of India.

SHUKRIAA—Thank you.

TANDOOR—A clay oven used to cook naan, as well as chicken and other meats.

TAVA—A griddle.

THALI, THALIA—A stainless steel tray with compartments for different dishes.

TULSI—Holy basil herb.

YAAR—A friendly way to refer to a man, similar to "pal."

FAITH IS THE BIRD THAT FEELS THE LIGHT

WHEN THE DAWN IS STILL DARK

—*Rabindranath Tagore*

CHAPTER

 **1**

I crouch close to the bittersweet straw in the cow-shed, last night's strange dream racing through my heart. The cows shuffle to make room as I steady myself and duck low along the floor. I pry my fingers under the heavy stone, pulling out the small wooden box.

My hands tremble as I lift the lid, carefully unfold Papa's last letter, and trace his address across the fragile yellow paper.

102 CONNAUGHT PLACE, ZANDAPUR

He's been working away for eight long months and I don't know why he hasn't written since the half-moon in May, *four* months ago. I brush away my salty tears with the back of my hand and, even though I know his letter by heart, read each word as if he were right here with me.

Dearest Asha,
The city is so different from Moormanali. It's busy and full of people. Working in the factory isn't too bad but I'd much rather be home with you all. I know you'll be studying hard at school and helping Ma. I miss you every day and promise I'll come back for your special birthday on Divali. Always remember that I love you,
Papa

I begin to refold the letter but the clang of the spare cowbell startles me. It's swinging from a hook in the far corner, where not a breath of air can reach it.

And suddenly I'm back in the frozen landscape of my dream, lost in the ice wilderness of the Himalayas. I press my back against Tulsi's steamy body and struggle to calm her; the cows are spooked too.

I put the letter in my pocket and follow the bell as it moves from side to side through the whisper-still air. Goose bumps spike my arms and beads of cold sweat prickle my forehead, even though the shed is blazing with heat.

I keep my eyes fixed on the bell, grab Papa's scarf from the shelf, and wind it around my neck. I breathe in his comforting scent to stop the panic rising . . . then the bell sounds again, this time even more loudly, echoing in the air like a death toll.

I'm about to run and tell Ma but stumble when I hear Jeevan outside shouting my name, his urgent footsteps pounding closer and closer. He bursts in, sending straw and dust flying everywhere.

"Asha!" His face is red-hot and fear sparks in his brown eyes. "Asha, come quick, your ma needs you."

"What is it?" I clutch the scarf. "You're scaring me."

"Just c-come." He's panting so hard that his words

burst out in snatches. "Something terrible is . . . I'll tell you on the way."

"Is Ma all right? Is she hurt? Tell me."

"We've got to get down there." He grabs hold of my hand, pulling me out of the shed, and we hurtle downhill to the village, but the path is steep and the loose stones are making me slip as air shoots into my lungs in painful gulps.

I squint toward the clutch of houses, shielding my eyes against the glare of the shiny solar panels, and just make out a group of people gathered around our gates. They look like little dots from here and I can't work out who they are.

When we get closer, I see Ma, her green chunni flying through the air like it does when she uses it to swat flies.

Jeevan grips my hand so tightly I can feel his fingernails, sharp on my palms.

"There's a woman and some men," says Jeevan between breaths. "Not from around here. They're asking for money from your ma."

I feel sick, press my side to stop the stitch, and keep

on going past the mango tree. We're only a few steps from my house now, where everyone is spilling out of the garden, and I see the people Jeevan told me about.

Two hulking men tower over Ma, and one of them is pointing a blunt metal pipe right in her face. A red car is parked outside too, with a slim woman dressed in Western clothes standing beside it. My blood turns cold.

"Jeevan, what's happening?"

"I don't know!"

We force our way through the crowd. The twins are clinging to Ma's legs and crying.

"Ma!" I shout over the noise. "Ma!"

She ignores me. She's trying to grasp the slim woman's hand. "One more month, Meena, please!" she cries.

The woman flicks Ma away. "I'm a businesswoman, not a charity," she says coldly. "Now . . . where's the money?" She nods to one of her men, the one with the pipe, who shoves Ma and sends her tumbling to the ground.

I rush to Ma's side while Jeevan pulls my little

brother and sister away from danger. His mother, who's watching with the other neighbors, scoops them both up. Ma stands and brushes the dust off her clothes.

The woman, Meena, signals to one of her men. "You search the house. I'll check the outbuildings. And you"—she points to the other man—"make sure no one interferes."

The man with the pipe kicks at our front door with his boot.

"Ma—*do* something!" I shout. Needles stab at my stomach.

But she looks the other way.

"Get away from our house," I yell, boiling with outrage.

The man bares his crimson teeth in a paan-stained smile, shoves aside the beaded curtain, and disappears inside.

Ma stands watching the door, frozen to the spot. Why isn't she doing anything?

I run into the kitchen, my legs shaking, Jeevan right behind me.

"You can't just walk into our house!" My voice cracks.

"Can't I?" The man turns and his jaw moves mechanically, still chewing the paan. He spits a bloodred line across the floor, filling the room with his putrid breath.

Jeevan charges toward him. "Stop! That's disgusting!"

A fierce admiration bubbles inside me as my friend and I exchange a look swift as a heartbeat. "Jeevan, be careful." I grab him by the arm. "Don't go too close."

The man's mouth twists into a strange grin as he drops the pipe on the floor. "Where's your papa when you need him?" he sneers. "Probably in some toddy shop spending all your money . . . and I bet he's never coming back."

"My papa doesn't even drink." I'm filled with anger. "And if he were here you wouldn't dare to come anywhere near our house."

He knots his eyebrows together over his beetle-black eyes and goes to the latticed cupboard door where Ma keeps the crockery. "Is this where you hide the valuable stuff?" He looks inside, but nothing in there is worth much. He sweeps everything out, knocking my best blue cup off the shelf. It clatters to the ground, smashing to pieces. He storms past Jeevan, who stumbles backward onto the floor.

"Leave him alone!" I cry, and without thinking throw myself at the man and kick him as hard as I can.

"You . . . little swine!"

He grasps me by the wrist and shakes me violently. When he finally lets go, my knees buckle as fear swamps me.

Ma runs in, pulls me toward her. "Please . . . stop this. We have nothing to give you. There's nothing valuable in here."

Ma's neck is bare and I realize they must have already forced the gold pendant from her.

Meena sweeps through the door and looks around, wrinkling her nose. She knows what she's looking for; her eyes catch on our brass pot. She reaches into it and brings out the key to the old tractor, which she must've seen in the back shed. "We'll take this as interest," she says to Ma, dangling the key for a moment before tossing it to her thug. "But I'll be back for the full repayment." She walks out of the house.

Interest? Repayment? The words spin around in my head but I can't make sense of them. The only thing I'm sure about is that she's taking the tractor.

"No! Not Papa's tractor," I shout after Meena, sprinting into the garden. "How will we do all the hard farm jobs?"

Meena is sliding into the driver's seat of the red car.

Her men climb onto the tractor. The engine starts with a splutter, followed by an ear-piercing screech.

"No!" I cry, unable to keep the sobs from escaping. "No!"

Meena winds down the window of her sleek car and fixes Ma with a stare. "We'll be back for the money by nightfall on Divali. If you don't have it, we're taking the house."

She accelerates out onto the road before Ma can reply, followed by the tractor.

"Ma!" I scream. "Don't let them steal it!" My words are drowned out by the engine noise and the neighbors' shouting.

Jeevan joins me and we run past Ma, past the neighbors, following the vehicles onto the road. My lungs burn and my legs ache. They're too fast. We can't stop them.

Jeevan swears at them, his face livid, his eyes full of fire.

His words shock me, even in this moment of hopeless fury, but I let them hang in the air.

The car and tractor head along the twisting road that leads away from the village, throwing dust onto the ripening barley fields, the engine noise getting fainter and fainter.

CHAPTER

2

One by one our neighbors leave, talking to each other in hushed voices. Jeevan and I walk together back toward the garden, so close that our arms touch, his eyes glistening. He turns his face away, brushing his nose roughly with the cuff of his sleeve.

My throat is tight and I can hardly breathe. The words "interest" and "repayment" echo through my mind as I realize what has happened. "How could she? How could Ma borrow money from that horrible woman?" I say under my breath.

"Try not to think about her." Jeevan leads me back

into our garden. Ma's talking to Jeevan's mother about Meena, shouting words I've never heard her say before, the kind you're not meant to say. They're laden with anger and grief and her face is all worn out.

"Let's clear up the mess," says Jeevan's mother, putting an arm around Ma's shoulder and leading her inside.

Ma's face is red with shame, tears streaming down her cheeks. "I didn't think she'd actually come here and threaten us like that . . . if Paras had been here she wouldn't have dared." She catches sight of me and Jeevan and tries to control herself.

"You're doing your best," says Jeevan's mother. "You weren't to know she'd just turn up like that."

"Asha," Ma says, wiping her face. "See to your brother and sister, please. I sent them off to the swing."

"I'll go," says Jeevan, blowing the hair off his face. "I can take them to our place, give them something to eat—you've got enough to deal with here." He shoots me a smile and I smile back gratefully.

Jeevan and I run over to where Rohan and Roopa are playing on the swing Papa made for us.

They leap off and wrap their arms around my waist. "Why were those men so angry?" asks Roopa.

"That lady was really mean," says Rohan, snuggling closer, "and they made Ma cry . . . I hate them."

"Some people enjoy being nasty; it makes them feel big and important. But don't worry—they've gone now and everything will be OK." I force a smile and try to sound confident but I'm beginning to doubt everything.

"Who wants a ride on my bike?" asks Jeevan. He picks the bike up off the ground and props it against the wall. Rohan and Roopa squeal as he lifts them onto the seat. "Hold on." He climbs on the crossbar and twists to face me. "We'll find a way to get the tractor back, I promise."

I watch them disappear out of the garden, feeling numb and useless, my throat so tight I can't speak.

How much has Ma borrowed? They said they'd be back at Divali—that's only seven weeks away. How will we get the money? All I can think of is what we'll do next time, when they come back again, and it fills me with darkness.

I look up. The mountains, far beyond the grazing grounds, make a black, jagged ridge against the setting sun.

When I go inside, Jeevan's mother has gone and everything is quiet.

The broken pieces of my blue china cup are piled one on top of the other. Ma hasn't thrown it away with the rest of the things that were broken, and I feel a surge of love for her. I pick up a shard, feeling the rough, cracked edge against my skin, and slip it into my kurta pocket.

Ma is sitting on the wooden bench, staring with bloodshot eyes into a hot cup of chai, her face puffy and her long hair—usually so neatly tied back—loose and wild.

"You've got to tell me what's been going on, Ma." My words are urgent and my insides are twisting up again. "Ma, look at me."

"I know you're worried and I promise we'll talk later." Her voice shakes and she passes a hand over her hair. "We need milk for supper, did you bring it down?"

"No, this is too important, Ma—don't change the subject. I'm not a child you can hide things from anymore."

"It's been such a dreadful day . . . I'm sorry, Asha." She speaks like she's in a trance. "Where are Rohan and Roopa?"

"Jeevan took them for a ride on his bike, remember? Drink a bit of chai, Ma, it'll make you feel better." I bite my lip. "What happened? Why did you borrow money from that woman?"

Ma doesn't speak. She gets up. "You know . . . we haven't heard from your papa for four whole months, Asha . . . I keep on waiting but there's been no letter since May." She spits each word out like a bitter seed.

"I know." I miss Papa more than if I'd lost my own arm or leg. "Ma"—I make her look at me—"everything will be all right. He wrote so many letters before. He loves us. He said he'd come back for my birthday, for sure. He's probably just been really busy with work." I have to convince her so she doesn't give up. "Just tell me the truth. Why did you borrow the money?"

She sits opposite me, dark semicircles around her

eyes. "I didn't want to tell you," she says. Her voice has lost its usual lightness and sounds as brittle as glass. "You know that we can't survive on the money we make from the farm—even with my extras it's not enough—and your papa . . ." She hesitates. "Asha, he hasn't sent any money since that last letter in May."

"What?" I nearly choke on the word, the reality of what Ma has said forcing me to grow up in a single breath. I grip the table, unable to speak. I knew about the letters stopping, but she never told me the money stopped too.

"I had nowhere else to turn," she says, using the edge of the tea towel to dab away her tears. "I kept thinking he was just running late, that the money would turn up the next month. But it never did." The sky grumbles and looks darker than ever. She wraps her arms around me and kisses me lightly on the head. "Stay inside—I should get the milk. I won't be long. I promise we'll talk more when I get back."

I wait for her to go, then trail into the back garden with its neat rows of shiny peas and peppers that she's been growing to sell at the market. The chickens are still unsettled and they can't stop squawking and pecking each other. Warm drops of rain splash onto my hair and trickle down my neck as I shelter under the wide-canopied shisham tree beside the house, its rough trunk hard against my back.

Glossy black-winged rosefinches with their blushed underbellies chatter and dive out from between the branches, chasing each other, dripping more rain from the leaves like holy water. I let it fall on my face, willing it to revive me, and think of a curse to hurl at the people who've invaded my home.

"Do not dare to return here, but begone to the northern poles where nothing grows except cruel ice, and place your heart beneath the white bear's claw, under the ghost wolf's foot. May you wane forever, shrivel like a coal on the fire, shrink like slime on the wall, waste away like a starving child and become as small as a drop of saliva from a fly's vomit and much smaller than a speck from the dung heap and so very tiny that you become nothing."

I slip onto the ground, letting my shoulders droop at last, exhausted by the burden of the day. I sit with my eyes closed, trying to make sense of what's happened, but it doesn't make any sense at all. Why would Papa stop sending the money? The rain has cleared the air and I breathe in the early evening smells: warm soil, grass, and the sweet star-shaped bakul flowers, like the ones that Papa collected for me last summer when we took a picnic high into the mountains instead of doing chores. He made them into a garland and crowned me queen of the Himalayas.

Is he safe? Has something happened?

The crickets begin their raucous clicking, droning their steady evening song like a chorus you can't blot out. I go back inside. I walk over to the small shrine we keep on a shelf in the kitchen and top up the clay deeva with mustard oil.

Striking a match, I light the deeva, just as I've done every single night since Papa left, and watch the pale yellow flame flicker dimly at first, then explode into a bright light, shining golden under the statue of Shiva, who looks so calm sitting there with his hand raised in peace. I take a deep breath and my senses fill with the comforting scent of jasmine from the garland Ma twined around his neck this morning.

"Maybe this will bring us some luck." I put my hands together and close my eyes. "Please, Lord Shiva, protect this house and all of us who live here. Protect my papa, wherever he is. Keep us safe and reunite us and give thanks for Jeevan and his family and our neighbors." A rush of fear fills my stomach. "A-and especially protect us from Meena."

When I open my eyes, I notice a letter tucked behind the statue. It's got a blue British stamp on it and must be from Uncle Neel in England. Why didn't Ma show it to me? She usually reads all his letters to us. My stomach turns a somersault; she's been keeping another secret from me! I slip the letter out of its envelope, reading hurriedly, with one eye on the door . . .

Dearest sister Enakshi,
We are all fine in England. London gets cold quickly in September. Not like India, where you must still be feeling the heat of the sun. The leaves are starting to fall and that means all the children are going back to school.

Manu begins his exams this year. We
hope he works hard...

I know you haven't heard from Paras
for so long, or received the money he
promised to send you. Do you think it's
time you thought about selling the
farm? You can have a good life here.
Be brave, Enakshi. Come to England...

My hand is shaking—I can't finish reading.

So this is what Ma's been planning! How can she even consider leaving Papa behind while he's working to keep us all alive? And what happens when he comes back and there's nobody here? With the letter still in my hand, I storm outside, gasping for fresh air.

I stand against the house, staring wildly into the sky. My heart won't stop slamming against my ribs and my breathing is out of control.

The stone wall is scorching with heat from the day and I lean against it. A single mottled toad shuffles out of the shadows and I kneel on the damp mud beside it, listening to its soulful croak.

Way above, a half-moon appears through the burnished evening clouds, lighting up the wings of a circling lamagaia—a bearded vulture—and for some reason it makes me think of Nanijee, Ma's ma, who died when I was six. Nanijee believed the spirits of our loved ones lived on through animals, and said that after she died she would come back to us and we should look out for her.

I close my eyes and don't feel quite so jumpy—the memories of my nanijee are tugging me back to earth.

You were such a tiny thing when you came from your ma, bloodied and bawling, hardly bigger than my outstretched hand. You fought your way into the world on that stormy night with the thunder thrashing onto the rooftops and lightning searing the skies.

Your mountain-green eyes shocked the whole village. You were the one chosen to carry forward the ancient name Asha . . . you were our hope and I clasped you in my arms.

When I open them again, the lamagaia has perched

on the old well. It's about the size of a lamb, with dark bronze wings and a gray beak. Golden feathers cover its head and the rest of its body. It struts around the crumbling wall and begins pecking as if it's looking for grains of wheat. Then it spreads its wings, which are far wider than my outstretched arms, and lands beside me, *right* there, on the ground. Even though its wings are now folded, the bird is colossal.

They usually keep away from people, but I'm so close I can see each bright yellow scale on its legs and its gray-ridged talons, which it uses to scratch at the ground.

The lamagaia starts to make a clucking sound, as if trying to tell me something, and I stare into its dark-flecked eyes, mesmerized. I feel a little heart patter of nerves but lean even farther forward, stretching my fingers toward its feathery wing. It hops away—perches back on the well, tilts its head to one side, and lifts its wings.

"I wish you *were* my nanijee," I say, my voice quivering. "I need her so much." A gray feather tinged with gold floats down and lands by my foot. I stroke its silky softness and weave it into my braid. "Perhaps I'll call you my spirit bird."

It keeps looking at me, unfurls its powerful wings again, and this time rises into the gray-white sky, billowing dried shisham leaves into the air like dust.

CHAPTER

3

A while later, Jeevan brings the twins home to find me crying at the kitchen table. I wipe my tears and help him to put my brother and sister to bed.

Afterward Jeevan places an awkward hand on my back. "Are you OK?"

I walk over to the shrine. "Jeevan, look." I push the letter from Uncle Neel in front of him and point at the bit about England. "Ma's been keeping this secret. Uncle Neel wants us to sell the farm and go and live there."

Jeevan's eyes dart to the floor, then back to me. "She

wouldn't actually think of leaving, though, would she?" He looks away. "Do *you* want to go?"

I beat back the tears. "How can you think I'd want to?" I say, folding my arms across my chest. "You know how much I love being here. Nowhere would be the same . . . and I'd never find a friend like you." I reach for Jeevan's arm and push the sleeve of his shirt away from his wrist to reveal a friendship band. "Remember the day I tied this?" My face burns as hot as coals as I recall how he stood up to those men, putting himself in danger. "Our friendship means the world to me, Jeevan! Especially now! Everything's tumbling around me and I don't know what to do."

"We made a pact to always help each other," says Jeevan, twisting the band. "And I mean to keep my promise."

I hear the sound of chappala squelching on the damp ground outside, and nervous jabbing pains stab my stomach. "Quick, it's Ma." My guilty fingers can barely fold the letter and I push it clumsily back behind the shrine.

Jeevan steps toward the doorway. "Meet me in the mango tree later."

"OK. I'll try to get away. Thank you."

He bumps into Ma as she brings in the milk. "Were you helping Asha with her homework?" She tries to smile and ruffles his hair.

He quickly smooths it back down. "Yes . . . something like that . . ." he adds under his breath, the secret turning his cheeks red. "See you tomorrow."

"Let's eat," says Ma, letting out a long sigh and striking a match to light the stove. "Call Rohan and Roopa, will you?"

"They already ate at Jeevan's," I say, desperate to talk about what's happened. "They're in bed. And I don't feel like eating . . . I just want to talk, Ma. What's happened to Papa? Why hasn't he sent the money like he promised?"

She still doesn't answer me but concentrates on ladling the yellow dhal into two wooden bowls and hands me the one with most. I shake my head and push it away.

"Come on, Asha. You have to eat. It's Monday

tomorrow and you've got school." She stands beside me, twisting the tea towel. "You know the sacrifices we've made so you get a good education . . . it's really important."

I grab hold of the tea towel so Ma has to face me. "What's the point of education if we're going to lose the farm and go to England anyway?"

She looks at me, nodding slowly. "So you found the letter."

I feel my cheeks redden.

"Sit down and eat something, Asha."

I throw myself onto the wooden bench and tear at a rock-hard roti leftover from this morning, dunk a piece viciously into the dhal, and shove it into my mouth, but it won't go down and scratches my throat.

"That's right . . . eat up." Ma's brow is set in a deep furrow as she pours a cupful of the milk and begins heating it. "This will give you some strength." She sprinkles cinnamon and places the frothy warm drink gently in front of me.

I sip at the milk, forcing the hard bread down my

throat. "Will they really come back at Divali?" I ask, afraid of what she's going to say. "And if they do, will we really have to sell the farm?"

Ma doesn't reply, she just clasps her hands together and stares at the doorway, and I know that the answer is yes.

"If only we knew where my ma hid her gold," she says after a long pause. It's as if she's in another world.

"Nanijee had gold?"

"She only told me about it when she was dying. She was feverish, so I was never sure how true it was."

"What did she tell you?"

"She said that it was a collection of all the precious gold dowries given to the daughters of our family. Each generation from way back added to the treasure and passed it on. She said there were ancient engraved bangles, earrings, necklaces. Your nanijee wanted to keep it all together and safe for hard times . . . but it was all so long ago that nothing is certain."

"Did you ever see it?"

"No," says Ma, twisting the tea towel again. "We don't know what she did with it. Maybe she intended to tell us, before she died—but she didn't get the chance. Or maybe it never existed at all."

"If we could find it"—I begin to feel excited—"Papa wouldn't have to do that awful job in the factory . . . and we wouldn't be forced to go to England."

"Don't you think we've looked, Asha?"

I will my heart to stop thudding, and take a deep breath. "Ma, we *can't* leave Papa behind. Anything could have happened to him. This is our home. He might come back here looking for us."

"I can't manage without him. I've been to Sonahaar to get a clear phone signal. I tried the number he gave us over and over again, but it's dead. And I keep sending letters, but no reply."

"We can't *abandon* him, Ma!" My words are choked and I can hardly get them out.

Ma's face clouds over. "But what am I meant to do?"

"Everything I love is here in India," I say between sobs. "I don't want to go to England, Ma."

But her expression is suddenly determined. "I don't want to either. But if we don't hear from him or receive any money by Divali, we won't have a choice. We'll have to sell the farm to pay Meena back. I'll tell Uncle Neel we'll come. That will be nearly six months without a word from your papa."

"Ma, we can't—that's only seven weeks away." I grip the edge of the table. "We can't leave him. I don't care what you say. I won't go, Ma! I won't!" I run out of the kitchen, Ma following behind.

CHAPTER

4

She finds me in the garden. All the anger has fled from my body and I feel drained. She brings me close to her and I bury my head into her shoulder. "I'm sorry about all this, Asha." She wipes the tears from my face. "But we have to do *something*." She leads me back inside and we stand beside the shrine. "Let's light another deeva, shall we?"

"Ma," I whisper, feeling more tired than ever. "Can you tell me the story of when I was born?" I need to chase away the memories of Meena and the men invading our home.

"But you've heard it so many times before."

She's smiling, though; she loves this story as much as I do. "Please, Ma," I say, pulling her onto the bench beside me.

"Well, OK," she begins. "The big Divali celebration, the festival of lights, was approaching. My ma, your nanijee, came to visit from her village in the far-off mountains and everyone lit their deevay, acting out the story of Prince Rama and his wife, Princess Sita, and their return home after being banished by the king, just like every year." Her face brightens. "Your papa was so attentive; we were very excited. Then out of the blue there was the most spectacular thunderstorm." Ma unbraids my hair as she speaks. The lamagaia feather falls into my lap, where I hold it carefully.

Ma picks up the comb, passes it through my hair. "You have such long, thick locks, Asha, just like Lord Shiva, so lucky . . . So that night nearly twelve years ago is when you decided to come into the world . . . and we called you the thunder baby."

"And what did Nanijee say when she saw my green eyes?"

Ma gives a deep sigh, as if she's really missing her

ma. "Nanijee took one look into your mountain-green eyes and said, *This baby will see things that others can't.*"

"And do you think that's true, Ma?" I sip some milk and trace the red pattern on the tablecloth with my finger.

"Everything can be seen in different ways," she says, sprinkling jasmine oil in my hair. "It all depends on what you believe in. You're growing up now; you have to start working things out for yourself." She notices the lamagaia feather in my lap and lays it on the table. "Where did you find it?"

"Out in the garden. Ma . . . how would you know what form the spirits of our ancestors take?"

Ma's voice fades into the background, and the answer comes from somewhere else.

Didn't I tell you, Asha, on that day when I left you? Lying still under the covers of fine white muslin, my breath beating out of me slow and labored. I called you to come and sit beside me and not to be frightened because I would never really leave you . . . my spirit soul would find a way back to you.

". . . If you look right into its eyes they say you can

gaze into its soul and tell if it belongs to your clan . . .
Are you OK, Asha?"

I lean against Ma. "Mmm."

Nanijee would have seen lots of lamagaias, because
of where she was born in the mountains, and it makes
me feel excited when I think of the one I saw earlier,
especially after my memory dream. "Ma, did Nanijee
ever talk about lamagaias?"

"She used to tell a story that she once found a lamagaia chick in an abandoned nest high on a mountain
ledge when she was looking after the family goats. She
watched it for a few days but no parent bird came to
feed it, so she took it little tidbits and reared it until it
became a fledgling. She said it got big really quickly,
even though it was still so young. She loved it and it
always came back to her even after it had grown up.
That's what she told me, anyway."

She rebraids my hair and puts the feather back.

Then she pulls a red silk purse out of a knotted corner of her chunni. "I took my pendant off to keep it
safe from Meena." She holds the purse tenderly. "And
I think it's time you had it . . . *my* ma gave it to me

when I was twelve and now it's your turn."

"I thought they'd taken it." I feel butterflies fluttering in my stomach and watch Ma as she brings it out.

The pendant is shaped like a teardrop with a curved tip and has a tiny red gemstone at the end. She unclasps the long chain and hangs the necklace she has worn for as long as I can remember around my neck.

I touch its surface, which is like fine gold lace, and wrap my fingers around it.

"Oh, Ma..." I can't find the right words. "It's... beautiful... I'm honored to have it and I promise to look after it forever."

"Your nanijee said to give it to you on your twelfth birthday, but I think you should have it now. It's been passed on through the generations, always to the eldest daughter. It's a very special gift, Asha." Ma holds my face in her hands. "The pendant is an ancient symbol called a buta," she says. "It comes from the northern Himalayas. That's where Nanijee's family came from, where your mountain eyes are from, and where the lamagaias originate."

She leads me to the mirror behind the shrine and

the pendant catches golden light from the flickering deeva, illuminating Ma's face behind me, and in this moment a rhythm sweeps through my body as if I'm connecting to all the daughters in my family who have worn it before me. It's as if I'm seeing my eyes properly for the first time, mountain green, flecked with fury, and the faces of my ancestors flash across them like stars from the distant past. The roar of a silent war cry thunders through my head—*I won't let the farm be sold, we won't go to England and leave Papa behind, no matter what Ma says!*

CHAPTER

5

I prop myself up in bed waiting for our signal, and there it is, a flashing light through the small window; Jeevan is already in the mango tree.

I rush onto the roof terrace, trying to stop my chappala flicking the stone steps as I pick my way down to the garden, duck past the window where Ma sits sewing, and slip through the gate. I hurry away from the house. The velvet night is filled with the haunting call of owls on the hunt. I reach our big rock at last and sprint past it toward the mango tree, filled with the promise of a plan.

I throw off my chappala at the base of the tree and slot

my bare foot into the first worn hold. Pushing through the rain-drenched leaves, I balance myself onto the branch next to Jeevan.

"What am I going to do?" I blurt out straightaway, my words strangled. I tell him everything that passed between Ma and me in a rush of words, and by the time I finish I'm nearly in tears. "And she said if we don't hear from him by Divali, we're going to go to England."

Jeevan touches the lamagaia feather. "What's this in your hair?"

"Oh . . ." For some reason the observation calms me down. "It's nothing, just a feather I liked the look of." I don't tell him what happened in the garden earlier, that I hope the lamagaia is the spirit of my nanijee, in case it breaks the spell I feel every time I think of her. He might say spirits can't exist . . . he might ask me: *How can you prove it?* And I know I can't.

"Jeevan, what do you think's happened to Papa?" I revisit all the possibilities I've imagined over and over again. "There must be a reason why he hasn't written." I force myself to say the words I haven't dared to speak, as if saying them aloud would release some demon's wrath and make them come true. "Do you think he's . . . forgotten us?" My heart speeds up at the final words.

"No. Don't say that. Your papa isn't like them."

We both know about men who go to the city to work but never, ever come back.

"I knew something strange was about to happen today," I say after a pause. "The bell in the cowshed started moving all by itself at the same time those men and that woman, Meena, were down at our farm . . . and I've started having dreams again." I turn to face him—I want to see how he'll react to what I have to say.

"You know how Nanijee thought I could see things that others can't?" I start slowly. "Well, last night I dreamt I was walking through the high Himalayas. It was so cold and snowy and I met an old woman. She let me warm myself by her fire." I look down at my palms. "She said I had a message in my lines."

I watch Jeevan's face closely before the moon disappears behind a cloud and we're pitched into darkness. But when he speaks again I can see that he's not taking me seriously at all. "It's just a dream, Asha," he laughs. "All sorts of weird things happen in dreams."

"Do you think I'm making it up?" My cheeks simmer with hot indignation.

"Calm down."

"You never believe me!"

"It's just . . . I can't see these things with my actual eyes, can I? Anyway, the really important thing now is to find out about your papa."

The moon reemerges, casting shadowy leaf patterns over Jeevan's arms, and for the first time I notice they've suddenly gotten as hairy as those of the boys in the upper school.

"Look, Ma gave me Nanijee's pendant today," I say, pulling it out to show him. "She said it was a special gift."

"Your ma must really trust you." He examines it closely, and his voice softens. "Maybe only someone special can wear such a gift."

I'm glad the moon is half-hidden behind the clouds so Jeevan can't see me blushing.

After a few moments he speaks again.

"Maybe you're right. Maybe your dreams *are* guiding you in some way." Jeevan picks a wide mango leaf and begins to crush it, releasing a mouthwatering sweet scent. "Even if it's just your instincts, a kind of psychology."

"Do you think so?" I stare up at the sky through the leaves.

"What do *you* think?" asks Jeevan.

I try to order my jumbled thoughts. "Ma says that now that I'm nearly twelve I have to start working things out for myself . . . I think the dreams *are* guiding me, but toward *what*? I need to focus."

A hushed silence falls inside the mango tree while we both think, the soft raindrops soothing my racing mind.

Eventually, Jeevan speaks. "You know the lonely house at the farthest end of the village?"

A chill makes the hairs on my arm stand up. "The witch's house?"

Jeevan nods. "Well, what if your dream is telling you to go and get your palm read? She can definitely do that!"

I'm surprised at Jeevan's suggestion. I thought he'd say palm reading is a load of nonsense.

We climb down from the tree and start the trek up the mountain, taking the long way around to the farthest end of the village and then even farther, where there's only one house for miles and it's hers.

The hot autumn wind catches at our ankles as if it's egging us on, tearing at the leaves in the trees. I can't help imagining some wild thing stalking our footsteps.

"I don't know about this . . . people say she spreads curses at night." My voice is quiet.

"It's just superstition, Asha."

"Then why are we going?" I whisper. He doesn't reply.

"Remember that boy Amir in the year above us?" I say, too jittery to look behind. "He said she digs up dead babies' skulls and uses them to conjure up their spirits."

"He was only trying to scare you," says Jeevan. "They're just stories, that's all."

I press myself closer to Jeevan as we skirt the edge of the mountain, following the moon, then cross my fingers behind my back as the house looms closer and we begin to drop down the hill.

I push the gate hesitantly, expecting it to be locked, but it swings open with a loud creak to reveal a tumble-down house with a straggly roof of twigs strapped to its beams. It's tucked into the far corner of a cavernous yard full of eerie black moon shadows. Our flashlight makes a halo of light ahead of us and we step cautiously toward it, my mouth dry and my stomach churning.

I can't believe I'm standing in front of this crumbling wooden door. It's like papery bone, bleached silvery white by the sun and rain.

"Do you want to go back home?" I ask, willing him to say yes this time. "We can still sprint to the gate. It's not too late."

"Let's get it over with." He speaks quickly, his voice shaking. "L-let's hope we find the answers you're looking for."

Was it right to come here knowing that this place might hold dangers?

A gust of wind billows behind us and a sudden clatter makes me look up toward the doorway. Beaks! They're strung together and suspended from a hook hammered into a stone alcove. And dangling by a thin, weathered rope is a skull, brimming with a powdery gray ash that floats onto the ground in front of us.

"Let's knock," he says. "Before we change our minds."

"I'll do it," I say, swallowing my fear and stepping up to the door.

"Use this." Jeevan picks up a large stone. "In case the witch has put invisible poison on the door."

I take the stone and bang loudly. The dull thud echoes into the dark night, cracking the silence of the yard. But nobody comes.

We wait, my heart thumping in my chest.

Just when we think no one's coming, the door flies open and we both leap back in horror.

CHAPTER

6

Perched in the low doorway is a woman barely taller than me, lighting up the darkness with the stub of a candle. Unfathomable musty smells billow out of the house.

I stay right beside Jeevan, square my shoulders, and try to control the beat, beat, beat of my heart pounding in my ears.

The woman's white hair is parted in the middle and twisted into a loose bun with a pointed black-and-white porcupine quill sticking out of it. She wears a green cotton sari, the loose fabric thrown over her skinny shoulder, the bottom of the fabric the same color as the ground, as if she's sprouted from the earth.

"Oh, look who it is," she says, flashing a row of crooked teeth like stunted tombstones. "It's the thunder baby and her friend."

Only Ma ever calls me that, so how does this old woman know my special name? My stomach folds in on itself and I suddenly wish I'd run back when I still had the chance.

"Chitragupta," she says, pointing to herself with a twisted fingernail. "So you want me to look at your palm, do you?"

Have I mentioned my palm? It's as if she's already reading my mind, and it sends fear coursing through me.

"Welcome." She beckons us into the house.

"No, Asha, let's not," whispers Jeevan. "Who knows what's in there? Let's make a run for it."

"No," I say, surprising myself. Thinking about Ma's words, I pull him into the house, even though my nerves are jangling and I'm more frightened than I can ever remember. "Come on, Jeevan, we can't turn back now. It's the only way I'll be sure what to do."

It's a hot night but strangely Chitragupta has a fire

burning in the hearth and something bubbling away in a heavy pot etched with ancient-looking writing.

We exchange a petrified look, staring with horror toward the pot. I grip Jeevan's arm, sliding myself as close to him as possible.

"Sit, sit," she says, pointing to a tattered woven bench on one side of the fire. She dips a steel cup into the pot and brings it out filled with . . . milky chai; it's not what I thought at all, but I still can't drink it.

"Shukriaa," I say politely. I hold the cup in my hand, not daring to put it to my lips. Jeevan isn't drinking his either, just looking down at the floor with his hands firmly clamped around the cup. He concentrates on holding it still, but the chai trembles.

"Yes," I say. "I—I need you to read my lines." My words come out slowly, as if I'm still unsure. "And tell me what to do."

"Drink a little chai first," she says, challenging us.

She stares so hard that I'm forced to take the tiniest sugary sip, and a strange herbal taste that I don't recognize clings to my tongue. What have I done? But before I can warn Jeevan, he does the same.

Chitragupta sits on her stool and gives a beaming smile in the semidarkness of the room, the candlelight and the fire showing the lines and wrinkles carved into her ghostly pale skin.

She pulls the porcupine quill from her bun, releasing a tangle of wild white hair, which floats around her face like writhing serpents. "Now," she says, her voice as crackly as wizened winter leaves crunched underfoot, "we are ready to begin." She throws back her head, grasps my hands, and begins stroking my palms. Her fingers feel like hot metal as she traces the lines I've studied over and over again.

Her voice is changed now. It's low and cavernous, coming from a place deep inside her. "Goddess of the Mountain," she says in a rumbling voice. "Reveal to us the sacred path that these friends must follow."

She studies my palms, narrowing her eyes. "You have a long journey ahead of you . . . I see snowy peaks that go higher and higher.

"You have been called by the Mountain Gods, my daughter. If you want your papa back, you must go and light a deeva at the most northerly temple of the

Himalayas at Kasare. This is important; it's where the Daughter of the Mountain, the Holy River Ganges, starts her journey."

A cool breeze fills the room and I hear gushing water, as if it's pouring out of a rock.

"Remember the story? When Lord Shiva had to slow the Ganges down and he laid his long hair in her way?"

She lifts my chin and forces me to stare into her eyes. They seem to spit out fire, making a high wall of flames between us. Roaring tigers spring out of the flames, snarling with sharpened white fangs, coming so close that their sour breath warms my skin.

I'm hotter than the time I had a fever and thought I was being chased by a pack of wolves. She tightens her grip on my hands and my head drops to my chest.

I feel like I'm in the middle of a dream with my eyes wide open, and I can't believe what I'm seeing but it's there as clear as day.

All around the edge of a magical circle, rows of dark green vines twist into the air. The room is filled with banyan trees with their long snakelike roots, giant figs dripping from thick stems. Blue-and-yellow Himalayan poppies wave in the gloom.

I want to know if Jeevan can see these things as well, but it's like my tongue has gone to sleep and it feels thick and useless.

"The Ganges made a great sacrifice by coming to the earth." Chitragupta's voice whirls into my head. "If you want your journey to go well, then you must make a sacrifice too . . . shave your head like a real pilgrim and wear orange and yellow for luck.

"The lamagaias will guide your journey. They are the spirits of your ancestors—they will watch over you."

She releases my hands at last.

"Asha, you must go on this journey; your papa is calling you."

I blink, and the fire, forest, and tigers vanish as suddenly as they appeared, leaving me chilled to the bone, as if I've been wandering through wind-torn woodlands and icy mountains forever. I bring my hands to my mouth and puff warm air into them but they are still frozen. I hold them above the fire, which sends out sparks and crackles like water being thrown into oil.

Chitragupta jumps off the rickety stool, sticks a long piece of wood into the leaping flames, and lights a bunch of incense sticks. Lifting them into the air, she swirls the smoke in white clouds around both of us.

The smell of spices mixed with strange animal scents in the small room make me giddy and I have to grip the edge of the stool to stop myself tumbling to the floor.

"You didn't know if you should come here or not, Asha . . . but it was right. I know you will use your powers for the good of others. Blessings for your journey."

"Asha." Jeevan yanks my arm. *"Come on!"*

We stumble toward the doorway as she scatters a handful of rose petals behind us.

"May the Gods smile on you, my children," she says, stepping outside. "I will watch as you go."

We sprint away through the yard as fast as we can, away from the house, with the breeze rattling the hanging beaks behind us. We don't stop until we're right past her gate, where we clutch each other and let out screams of hysterical, high-pitched laughter.

CHAPTER

7

I can tell Jeevan is properly spooked. "Let's get away from here," he says, grabbing my arm. "How did she know all those things?"

"I don't know," I pant.

"And when her voice changed," cries Jeevan.

"I thought we were going to die! It was all so weird . . . like a dream." My thoughts tumble over each other. "But something's changed in me, Jeevan. After everything that's gone on today, the thing that I know in my heart is that it's up to *me* to find Papa." I tilt my head back to look at the stars and feel like the ground is tipping beneath my feet.

I feel myself drifting, like I'm being tugged back in time by a silver thread.

You are like the warrior goddess Durga from the ancient texts, the wife of Lord Shiva who rode on a tiger and fought off the demons. Prepare yourself for a journey where the snow can fall deeper than the pines and the frozen mists swirl so thickly you can lose yourself for days . . .

"Asha. Are you OK?" Jeevan's voice makes me start. The memory splinters and is gone.

"Yes . . . just feel a little weird," I reply, trying to get my thoughts together. "I have to focus on how I'm going to find Papa."

"I've got an idea." Jeevan sounds excited. "We're going to the market in Sonahaar on Saturday—we're taking the cart and some cotton to sell. You could hide in it . . . if you're ready to go so soon?"

My body tingles with fear and excitement. "Yes . . . I think I *am* ready," I say. "Especially after everything Chitragupta said." I imagine the two of us setting off, through the wild Himalayas to Zandapur, and I sense a faint rhythm from my pendant.

"Papa usually loads the cart and keeps it below the

shelter out of the rain. You could get under the covers once it's dark, and in the morning I'll be there, driving the bullocks with Papa, making sure you stay safe."

"And *you* know all the names of the stars, so if we have to travel by night you'll know exactly how to navigate." It's all making sense and falling into place.

Jeevan puffs up, taking control again. "And once Papa's busy we'll find the train station and get going on our journey." He's speaking quickly, like he can't wait to get started.

"We can take the map of India that Papa left me," I say. "And mark the trail on it so we know exactly where to go."

"We'll get it all sorted," says Jeevan, rushing forward. "But let's hurry. It's getting late, and you know we've got old Mrs. Malhotra for math tomorrow."

I make a face. "And I haven't done my homework."

"Don't worry, just copy mine in the morning . . . as usual."

"And you can copy my English," I say, shoving him gently. "As usual!"

The pendant rocks against my collarbone as we

climb away from the witch's house toward the grazing pastures. "You're such a good friend, Jeevan. I know exactly what I have to do now and, just like Ma said, I'm working things out for myself, making my own decisions." I feel an invisible force, like a powerful hand pulling me toward my destiny. "Divali is only seven weeks away and I'm going to Zandapur to bring Papa home before Ma can take us to England."

CHAPTER

8

The week zooms by as fast as a flickering sunbird's wing and I can't believe it's Friday evening already; tomorrow, before the sun rises, we'll be gone.

Ma's writing something at the table when I come in from doing my chores. "You stayed out really late and . . . look at you." She quickly folds the paper over and pushes it into her pocket.

"I had to go back and rub some butter on little Sunny's hoof," I explain as water from my braid drips down my neck.

"You're soaking." She grabs a towel and wraps it

around my shoulders. "Come and sit with me." She's trying to sound cheerful, but the circles around her eyes look even darker than they did yesterday.

I touch the stitches on the kurta she's been making for someone in the village. "You're so clever—it's so neat, Ma."

"That's sweet of you. I can teach you to make one when we have some time."

I give Ma a tired smile. Going to Zandapur will make things worse for her; I know she'll be desperate with panic when she discovers I've left, and there won't be anyone to help her and she'll have to do everything all by herself, but I hope she'll understand that I'm doing this for all of us.

"Come," she says, taking my hand. "Let's go." She leads me up the stairs.

Rohan and Roopa breathe noisily on their side of the room, and just this once I'm glad they're asleep so I can have Ma all to myself, one final time.

The sheets are soft under my chin as she tucks me into bed. "Like when you were a baby . . . do you remember the little rag doll I made for you?" She touches my hair and hums distractedly. "The storm's taken some of the heat out of the evening so you'll sleep well tonight. Goodnight, dear little Ashi."

How she'll fret when she sees my empty bed in the pale morning light. "Goodnight, Ma. Could I have a hug?"

"Come here." She snuggles me close and I breathe in her smell—oniony, mixed with the heady scent of jasmine.

I cocoon myself against Ma's body, not wanting her to let me go. "What would I do without you?" she says, her eyes watery. "You've had to grow up too quickly these last few months."

Ma's words hit me hard—what *will* she do without me? I burrow my head deeper into the comfort of her arms and we stay like this until I feel myself drifting off to sleep. Eventually I hear the door click as she goes to bed, and I'm left flitting in and out of dreams, late into the guilty night.

I wake in a sudden panic and sit bolt upright. Is it time to go? I check the alarm clock by my bed but there's still half an hour to wait. My mouth is dry, my breathing fast, and I can hardly believe that I'm leaving home today.

In the hushed darkness of the room, I kneel on the bed, feel for the map of India on the wall, and pull it off.

I flick on my flashlight and lay the map out, but Rohan turns in his bed and I freeze, holding my breath. He wakes and calls out to me, like he does in the middle of the night. "Asha?" He sits up, rubbing his eyes. "Asha, what are you doing?"

"Shhh . . . nothing, you're just dreaming, go back to sleep," I whisper, hurriedly patting his cheek and kissing his clammy hand. "I . . . It's only a dream."

I hold my breath tight, watch his chest rising and falling, before I dare gasp for air again.

I go back to the map and begin to mark my route, the sharp flashlight beam spreading long shadows across the paper. The city of Zandapur is on the other side of the mountain—Papa circled it for me before he left—and we have to go through Galapoor first and then Kasare to get there.

Papa caught the train from Sonahaar, so I use my pen to mark it on the map, then finally find our village, Moormanali, and put a large heart shape around it.

I hastily get ready to write my messages for Ma but my hand hesitates—she says it's wrong to lie, but perhaps it isn't a lie. After all, I'll light a deeva once I get to the temple at Kasare. Trying to control my shaking hand, I begin the note I'll leave on my pillow . . .

Ma—I've gone to light a deeva for us all at the temple.
See you later—Asha

She won't think anything's wrong when she reads it—it's just the sort of thing I'd do on a Saturday morning—but when I start the second note, the one I'll leave under the statue of Shiva, the one Ma won't find until much later, I have to swallow hard.

Dearest Ma,
Please don't be angry. I don't want to go to England and the only person who'll stand

up and defend the farm is Papa, so I've gone to find him and bring him home. You told me to make my own decisions and this is what I have to do.

Don't worry, Nanijee's pendant will protect me.

All my love,

Asha

Ma will be shocked, tearful...and angry. She'll know I've lied to her, but I bite my teeth together, fold the notes, and put them on the bed.

I yank on the stiff jeans and hoodie Uncle Neel sent last year and tie the laces on my blue sneakers. These clothes will be a good disguise, in case anyone comes looking for us. I take the piece of broken cup from my kurta and slip it into my pocket.

I weave the lamagaia feather back into my braid, collect everything I'll need for my journey, and pile it all into my red bag.

I know Rohan and Roopa will cry when Ma tells them what I've done, but maybe they'll be impressed as well—they want Papa back as much as I do. I swipe my eyes. "Look after each other and be good for Ma," I say softly.

I stumble down to the dark kitchen, shining the flashlight ahead of me. The wooden door to the food cupboard scrapes as I open it. I flick a nervous glance over my shoulder, scooping a mango and two boiled eggs into my bag.

Even in this dusky light the statue of Shiva glows golden. I slide the second note under his foot. "Please, Lord Shiva," I whisper, quickly pressing my palms together. "Bless my journey. Look after Ma and Rohan and Roopa."

I pick up the matches and take them as well. We'll have to light fires when we sleep outside, to keep all the wild animals away.

The thought of the mountain wilderness filled with wolves and ravenous tigers makes my skin tingle, sending a shot of fear searing through my body.

CHAPTER

9

Leaving our house behind me, I run light-footed through the amber-smudged night toward Jeevan's farm buildings, blood pounding loudly in my ears. Once I reach the crest of the hill, I hunker behind the row of shivering neem trees, just in case his papa's arrived early.

I peer around the tree to check it's all clear and cautiously trip the final few yards to the shed, but Jeevan's already there, pacing backward and forward in front of the loaded cart.

"Everything OK?" I ask, trying to read his expression in the low light.

His forehead is creased with worry. He slides his eyes away from me, clasps his hands together, then blows the hair off his face.

I will my heart to slow down. "What's the matter, Jeevan? Something has happened, hasn't it?" My palms are sweaty and I'm afraid of what he's about to say.

He begins quietly. "I'm really sorry. I've thought about it over and over again, but . . ."

"But what?"

"I can't go with you."

"What did you say?" The night air suddenly feels heavy and I find it hard to breathe.

"If anything happened to me, Ma wouldn't know what to do."

"I don't understand, Jeevan. I thought you were my best friend . . . I thought you would do anything for me."

He tries to put his arm around me but I push him away and storm outside.

My face is burning. "I don't need you." The words we both know aren't true hang awkwardly in the midnight air.

"Y-you remember what happened to my brother."

"Yes . . . you told me." Jeevan's younger brother caught a fever when he was five and the doctor didn't get there in time. I know I should say something to make him feel better, but I just can't.

"I can't leave my ma like he did," he says, hugging his arms around himself and leaning against the shed.

Neither of us speaks.

"How will *my* ma cope if anything happens to *me*?" I say in a loud whisper. "Then she won't have Papa *or* me!" I remember her silence at supper and the way her tears were just a blink away. I turn my back on him, my throat aching from holding down a sob.

Then my anger explodes. "How dare you? You practically forced me to go to see the witch, you told me that I have to find Papa, and now . . . now at the last minute you're leaving me to do it all by myself!" I swivel around and punch him in the arm, hard, then look at the ground to stop myself from crying.

"Ow! Stop it! Look, I'm sorry, Asha." He holds me by the shoulders and tries to turn my face toward his. "*Look* at me."

But I struggle out of his grip and stomp away.

I'm shaking now, unable to see anything but a watery veil, and I sense my heart forming a tight fist against anything that he might say to make himself feel better.

"I promise I'll help your ma and look after Rohan and Roopa as if they were my own little brother and sister. I . . . I won't let that Meena woman or her thugs anywhere near the farm."

I keep my arms firmly crossed, refusing to speak.

"Maybe when we get to the market I could give you a signal to get away?"

I close my eyes and clasp my pendant. *Nanijee, if you're listening, help me to be strong, help me on this journey.*

Jeevan searches in his bag and hands me a map.

I shove it away. "Don't worry, I've got my own." My voice trembles. "I measured everything carefully . . . I don't need yours."

"Oh . . . suit yourself, then." He takes a few steps toward the path leading away from the sheds and turns as if to go, then twists around to face me. "Do you want it or not?"

I edge a little closer, peering at him from under my lashes, watching as he opens up the map under the nearly full moon. The paths are highlighted in different colors and there are funny little pictures to cheer me up along the way and he's even put our favorite constellations in.

But when he pushes it toward me, I still don't take it, so he rolls it up and puts it into my bag. I stay stubbornly silent but leave it there.

"I don't know if you want it, but I brought you this." He holds out the penknife his papa gave him for his last birthday. "It'll come in handy, and you'll need it more than me, and I sharpened some sticks for you, just in case you need weapons."

I reluctantly take his offerings, but my furious disappointment glows like a burning coal at the back of my throat and all I can do is shrug like I don't care anymore.

His face is rigid, as though he's trying hard to keep his feelings from spilling out. "I put a blanket in the cart to make it softer . . . I'll be back in an hour or so and I'll make sure you get away once we're in Sonahaar.

You'll do it, Asha; you're strong. Remember it's written in your lines."

He leaves me alone, surrounded by the vast night sky. Part of me wants to follow him, run home as fast as I can, wake Ma up and tell her how much I love her. I only wish he'd turn back, call and tell me he's changed his mind, but he's gone and I only hear the chilly mountain wind whistling down the valley.

The village houses down in the hollow cling to each other in the ash-gray light, shadowy ghostlike figures shrouded in the heavy mist.

I'm not sure I believe any of Chitragupta's predictions now . . . it's just me, no one else.

My insides are jangling with nerves, but I'm doing what Ma told me to, working things out for myself, making my own decisions. I grasp my pendant and sense its energy and rhythm releasing an invisible force, as if I'm reaching back across time, touching ancient spirits.

I find my words again at last and they fly from the embers, like a phoenix rising, filled with renewed strength.

I shake my hair free and feel the icy breeze blowing it back. "I'm Asha, with the mountain-green eyes," I howl. "I'll ride like the fearless warrior goddess Durga on the back of an amber-striped tiger, shooting flame-hot arrows, unleashing my anger against injustice. I will bring my papa home."

CHAPTER 10

The cart tips forward, the reins flick, and we begin moving. My insides churn like milk turning to butter.

I lift the cover an inch and peer out at sleepy Moormanali one final time from between the layers of cotton plants. Everything is the same as always, except that I'm leaving now, just like Papa did all those months ago when I buried my face into his jacket that smelled of all the smoky fires we'd ever built on the mountainside and begged him to hurry home.

The moon and the stars shine above me, just like they did for him, hopeful beacons, sending their blessings for the first day of my journey. I can't tear my eyes away from the fields of sugarcane cloaked in the secret light of earliest morning. I watch until my village gradually becomes a tiny distant hill, embroidered with everything I've ever known and loved.

The cart rattles on until I lose all sense of how long we've been on the road, but I'm sure Ma will have found my first note by now, telling her I've gone to pray for us all at the temple. This will please her, but later when she goes to light the deeva and finds the second note, she'll know I've lied, and I push the image away.

The cart suddenly jolts forward and I have to stop myself from calling out as my head crashes against the side. The revving motors and beeping horns outside drill into my brain.

I hear feet hit the ground and then a burst of raucous voices. Twisting onto my front, I shuffle toward the corner, ease up a little section of the cloth, and look out.

We're parked in front of a dhabba stall, like the one we all went to for Ma's birthday a long time ago, and the stallholder is pouring rice batter onto a massive tava, getting ready to make crispy dhosay for breakfast. The spicy potato filling that he's scooping up to stuff onto round, flat pancakes sends grumbles through my stomach, particularly as I spy Jeevan tucking into a huge one.

Just when I start to wish I'd given him another thump last night, I see a long paper straw being pushed beneath a corner of the cover. I grasp it with my fingers and yank it toward my mouth; fresh coconut milk! It slips down my parched throat.

For the first time since Jeevan let me down, I feel the ice around my heart thaw a little toward him, but in the next beat I remember his broken promises and the fury returns.

Once we're in Sonahaar I'll have to fend for myself, against anything that comes my way, and the thought makes my anger flare again.

I barely have time to squeeze back under the covers before we start to move again, the bullocks' hooves clattering along the cobbles toward the market, the bitter smell of gas fumes leaking through the covers, catching the back of my throat. We're getting closer.

We stop suddenly and I hear a thud as Jeevan and his papa jump onto the ground. There's a rustling and the sacking opens, flooding light into the cart. I sink back as far into the cotton as I can, making myself small, fear winding itself around me, anchoring me to the spot.

"You take them a bit of cotton, Papa, then I'll carry the rest over if they want it. I can manage."

It's only Jeevan . . . I let out my breath at last and settle back amid the itchy cotton, listening to the voices turn quiet, waiting for the signal he said he would give me.

I stay rigid, not daring to move for what seems like forever, and just when I think he's forgotten, he lifts the flap.

"It's all clear," Jeevan whispers.

My arms and legs are like lead and won't move until I force them out from under me, willing them into action. I feel for my bag and manage to slide out of the cart, landing in a twisted heap on the hard ground, my body on fire, the pins and needles nearly making me cry out. I pull up my hood and hobble into the busy market, desperate to get away without being spotted.

It takes all my willpower not to turn back and look

for Jeevan, but I keep my eyes straight ahead and slip away among the stalls, disappearing deeper into the labyrinth, my pendant bouncing in time with my heart.

I try my best to dodge the early-morning shoppers as they barge their way down the narrow aisles. A cyclist frantically rings his bell and yells over my head as he zooms past me, knocking me right into a woman dressed in a beautiful sari. She's carrying a garland of pale jasmine flowers as if she's going to the temple and has a delicate red bindi in the middle of her forehead.

"Careful, betay," she says kindly. She smells of freshly baked naan and my stomach gives an ache as she reminds me of Ma.

I take out my map and hold it in front of me, peering at the heart I drew around Moormanali this morning and the distance to Zandapur stretching between the two places. "Chai," cries a loud voice to my left. "Hot, hot chai." The boy is about my height and has a metal carrier in his hand full of clinking glasses and steaming pepper-spiced tea. He crashes into me, sending the map flying into a deep puddle. My hood slips off my head as I dive into the water after my map, the coils of my long braid unraveling. "Look where you're going, you spooky-eyed idiot. You nearly made me spill the chai and lost me my morning money." The boy mumbles more curses, heading off into the tightly packed stalls that spiral on forever.

"Sorry . . . I didn't mean to," I call after him. "It was just an accident." I lift the soggy map out of the puddle. The ink has run and the paper disintegrates in my hands. What use is it now? I leave it on a pile of empty boxes.

I duck into a wooden hut with a swinging sign that reads TOILET and take a deep breath of rotten air, trying to work out where to go and what to do next. What if Jeevan's papa has found out and comes chasing after me? And once Ma realizes I've gone, she'll call the police. I have to find some way of disguising myself.

I tug down my hood, run my hand along my braid, and know I have to give it up. I won't cry—it's only hair; it's not worth crying over—but when I think of all those years that Ma spent combing and oiling it, willing it to grow longer, thicker, more silky, I have to grab Jeevan's penknife quick before I lose my courage. I flick it open and hack into my braid. The hair is thick and hard to cut, the blade sawing backward and forward, painfully pulling at the strands.

The feather I wove back in this morning falls out and floats to the floor.

"This sacrifice is for you, Papa."

I pick the feather up, thread it through my chopped-off braid, and put it in my bag, ready to release it like Shiva did into the newborn waters when I arrive at the source of the Ganges.

I kiss my pendant, take the penknife one final time, and continue to hack my hair even shorter.

CHAPTER

11

I look in every direction before racing away from the stalls, heading out of the market toward a sign for the train station.

The sun bakes the back of my head and I think of Ma, who will be busy with the twins or cooking by now. She'll probably be making my favorite spiced eggy bread that I cover in oozing honey from our own hives. She won't go to light the deeva until later, so she won't have seen my second note yet. She'll think I'm on the mountainside, or tending the cows, not here in the middle of Sonahaar, running away from home.

I begin to cross the chaotic road toward a neem tree

in the middle of an island with traffic blaring all around it. The air is thick and smoky.

Taxis beep at meandering cows and a rickshaw driver nearly runs straight over me. When I reach the island at last, I leap toward the tree, clinging to it and wiping the sweat off my face.

On the opposite sidewalk is an old stone building with a sign above the wide double doors: SONAHAAR RAILWAY STATION.

I launch myself back into the road until I'm right by the doorway, where two dogs skulk, their heads low to the ground, chewing on scraps of paratha that some kind passenger has thrown to them.

I hope I don't come back as a dog after I die, having to beg for my food. Our holy teachings say you never know what animal you might become in your next life. I think of Nanijee and the lamagaia in the garden and wonder if it really was her.

I push the enormous doors open and step into a huge, echoing hall with a high glass ceiling. The station is full of people carrying heavy suitcases and immense bundles of luggage on their heads.

Hundreds of noisy sparrows fly from side to side, bickering and pecking at the ground.

I see straightaway that the hall is filled with police and keep my eyes lowered, turn briefly to check that no one is following me, and edge myself into the crowds. I'm swept along toward the far end of the hall with everyone else and stare blankly at a tall board with a list of place names I've only ever seen on a map or in geography lessons. I know I need to get to Galapoor, but I can't find it anywhere.

Even though it's sweltering in here, I feel too shy to pull my hood off, but my head is getting hotter and my thoughts spin around me in confusing spirals. Perhaps I need to find a train that's going toward the high Himalayas and stops at Galapoor or perhaps there's another board in another part of the station.

I squat on the ground with my back against a cool pillar, trying to work out what I should do as I stare at the list of destinations again. I'm begrudgingly grateful for Jeevan's map now and get it out, spread it on the ground, and find all the places that he measured and marked in different colors.

Compared to mine, his is so detailed. His numbers are a messy scrawl but I can see he's written that it's four hundred miles to Zandapur from here, and I feel my anger flash again as I think of his betrayal and cowardice for letting me do this all by myself.

I'm still studying the map when I get a strange feeling that someone is watching me. I peer around the pillar into the crowded hall but can't figure out who it might be. Maybe Jeevan's papa found out and went to the police; there are plenty of them about. My heart clatters noisily against my ribs.

I yank my hood forward, trying to bring it as close to my face as I can, and move toward the busier part of the station, keeping my head lowered.

I sense someone close behind me and I get ready to sprint, but a hand on my shoulder stops me.

I twist around. Is it the police? "Leave me alone!" I shout, ready to defend myself as best I can.

"Asha . . . Is that you?"

I can't believe it . . . a tight knot forms in my throat. "Jeevan! What are you doing here?" I push back my hood to take a proper look at him.

"I've been looking for you for ages. I wasn't sure it was you."

"So there *was* someone watching me!"

"I thought and thought about it." He twists at his friendship band. "And in the end I couldn't let you go by yourself . . . so when my papa was busy I came to find you."

I hurl my arms around him, hugging him as tightly as I can.

Jeevan turns beet red, waves his arms around to stop himself from toppling over, and clears his throat. "I'm sorry I let you down," he says quietly.

"I know how hard it must have been," I say. "But you came in the end and that's all that matters now."

A little frown appears between his eyebrows and I know he's thinking about what he's done, wondering how his papa will explain it to his ma when he gets home. "After I watched you leave, I kept imagining all the dangers out here," says Jeevan. "And I couldn't let you face them all alone. It'll be like that book we read at school, *The Three Musketeers*. 'All for one and one for all.'"

"There are only two of us," I say, laughing for the first time in ages. "In case you haven't noticed." Now that he's here, I feel a fresh surge of energy. "How do you like my new look?" I redden as I pass my hand over my clipped hair. Jeevan hasn't said anything yet.

"It looks . . . different," he says. "In a sort of interesting way, like a proper pilgrim." He smiles.

"Or a warrior," I add.

He suddenly starts to pace. "Let's go. My papa's probably noticed that I've gone. He might be looking for us and I'm sure he'll go to the police."

We push ourselves into the crowds of people waiting on the platform.

"We have to find a train that will drop us at Galapoor," I say.

"Ask someone. Look for a friendly face." Jeevan glances toward the doors.

"What about him?" I point at the first person who catches my eye.

Jeevan jumps in before I can say anything. "Excuse me, my ma wants to know which train goes into the high Himalayas from here."

"We need to get to Galapoor," I add.

The man points at the busy board. "It's the one that's going to Shimbala in half an hour," he says, looking us up and down. "Going for the fresh mountain air, are you, you and your brother?" He nods at me as he says "brother."

"Yes," says Jeevan quickly.

My cheeks feel red, but I'm pleased my short hair is fooling people. "Thank you," I say, smiling.

We walk away quickly and head toward the buzzing platform.

"I can't believe that man thought you were a boy," says Jeevan, elbowing me. "He must be half-blind."

I shrug. "It just means the disguise is working."

"Anyway, how are we going to get on?" asks Jeevan, changing the subject. "I didn't bring any money."

I look in my purse. "I haven't got much and definitely not enough for two train tickets. We'll have to sneak on. There are so many people they might not check."

All over the platform, frightening-looking guards in dark uniforms order the crowds about, directing them to trains, taking tickets, working through the chaos.

Jeevan's eyes widen as he watches them. "Those guards have got batons. What happens if we get caught?"

"I don't know," I say, making tight fists. "But I know we have to try and get on that train."

CHAPTER
12

We try to make ourselves invisible by pressing into the platform wall, keeping well away from the guards who stalk up and down like hungry wolves, ready to pounce, checking tickets—tickets we don't have.

"Come on, come on," I say, willing the train to appear. "If it doesn't come soon the guards are bound to spot us."

"As soon as it gets here, we'll fool them by jumping on in the middle of a crowd," says Jeevan, shifting around impatiently.

At last, a crackly announcement from the speaker blares on the platform.

"Train to Shimbala arriving next. Stand back, stand back."

My heart begins to pump wildly as the heaving and chugging train pulls into the station, hundreds of waving hands sticking out of the small square windows. The train hisses and screeches as it comes to a standstill, the iron wheels sending sparks into the air.

"Come on, Jeevan—quick, while they're all busy." We merge into the crowd as it surges toward the opening doors and begins squeezing into the carriages.

"Keep close to me," I gasp, clinging to Jeevan's sleeve. "We mustn't lose each other."

The rest of the passengers begin climbing aboard too, shoving their bags, suitcases, and bodies into us so I can barely breathe.

I propel myself toward a family right in front with lots of children. "Let's get on with them."

"OK . . . let's go," says Jeevan in a muffled voice.

"Tickets, please, tickets, please," someone barks in front of us, just as we're about to step on.

A uniformed guard takes one from the father in front and peers at it. "How many?" he asks. "Those two boys as well?"

The man glances at us, then puts his arms around his children. "Only these," he says.

The guard waves them in and fixes us with a scowl. I'm filled with fear and disappointment. "And you?" The guard lowers his face. "Where's yours?"

I pretend to search in my pockets for the ticket I know isn't there.

"It must have fallen out," I say, looking at Jeevan.

"Fallen out?" The guard makes a disgusted face. "More like never bought; now, get off." He spins me around and places his hand in the base of my back, pushing me off the train and back into the crowd, making me knock into a woman carrying a basket of fruit, which tips all over the ground.

"Hey, watch where you're going," she shouts angrily.

I begin to pick up some of the fruit but Jeevan tugs me by the sleeve and pulls me away from the woman, who swipes at me. "Let's get out of here," he urges.

We shove our way through the hordes. "What are we going to do now?" I ask, full of frustration. "We *must* get this train." I look up and down the platform. One end is much emptier, with hardly any guards. "Come on."

We hurry toward the quieter end of the platform and stop beside some carriages that don't have any windows.

"These must be for cargo," says Jeevan, jumping at the sound of the whistle.

"Jeevan!" I shout. "The train's leaving. We have to get on."

We run beside it as it jolts forward and stops.

"Quick." I force my fingers into a small gap in one of the doors and yank with all my force, but it won't budge.

"Move!" shouts Jeevan, trying to prize it open.

"No, let me. My hands can fit in the gap." This time I shove until my face turns hot and feels like it's about to explode. "One, two, three." I strain one more time and the door rolls open, stabbing splinters into my skin. I press my palms into the carriage and heave myself in, Jeevan following closely behind.

"Urgghhh!" he pants, lying on his front. "We did it!"

We push the door closed again and, despite the bright sun outside, there isn't much light in here. A dank smell of wet straw hangs in the air, and in the shadows there are dark shapes pushed against the back of the carriage—sacks, I realize.

"Let's hide behind these," I say, just as a shrill whistle sounds in the distance. We stoop behind the sacks, and a low shudder vibrates through the floor as the train picks up speed and rattles over the tracks.

Jeevan grins at me.

My body fills with excitement and fear. "We're going to find Papa . . . at last." I kneel behind the sacks and watch the whitewashed buildings of Sonahaar flash by through the small crack in the door. "And we'll face all the dangers together."

Jeevan digs into his bag, pulls out a green banana leaf package, and hands it to me.

"Look what I brought you from the dhabba stall."

I unwrap the large ridged leaves as carefully as if it were the best present in the whole world. "So you *were* thinking about me." I cram the spicy pastry into my mouth, the salty potato filling melting on my tongue. "This is so good . . . thank you," I mumble, savoring the last mouthful.

"I think you should twist your hair into a topknot,"

I add. "It's gotten so long recently. Then we'll both look different."

Jeevan pulls his hair off his face and holds it up. "What do you think? My ma always wanted me to grow my hair and be a good Sikh boy."

I give him the band from my braid and he ties his hair up.

Sweat suddenly slicks my palms. As if from nowhere, a horrible thought flashes through my mind. "What if the police track us down before we reach Papa? We'll be in such trouble and all for nothing."

"We can't let that happen," says Jeevan, squeezing my arm. "We'll find your papa and everything will be OK. You'll see."

CHAPTER

13

My head is heavy with sleep as the train follows the long, slow curve of the steep mountain path, creaking higher and higher, jolting me awake. The golden light from the setting sun hooks into the crack and spreads like honey into the carriage.

Ma will definitely have found my second note by now. She'll wonder why I haven't lit the deeva at the shrine and go to do it herself, and when she looks down at Lord Shiva's foot she'll wonder who's slotted a piece of paper under it. She'll let out a scream and Rohan and Roopa will start crying and ask where I've gone.

I reach into the pocket of my jeans and pull out the

piece of broken cup. I feel its rough surface. "I'll make you proud, Ma, and be back soon with Papa."

Jeevan's fallen asleep, his back resting awkwardly against one of the sacks. His mother will be waiting for him to come back from Sonahaar, and his papa will probably be searching for him through the streets. But we have to be each other's family now, and I'll look out for him like I know his little brother would have, his brother who died before Jeevan even had a chance to get to know him properly.

I take a peek outside at the jagged snow-crested mountains as they stretch upward into the sky, toward Galapoor and the wildernesses of the high Himalayas.

Papa told me it's the land of amber-eyed tigers and snow leopards, and when it rains in our village in the foothills, it snows up there. Sometimes, he said, the snow falls unexpectedly, in gigantic drifts, especially at this time of year, trapping people for weeks.

I feel a sudden panic and try to imagine how we'd ever survive under the layers of snow.

. . .

The train begins to slow down, its brakes finally screeching as it comes to a sudden halt. Perhaps we're in Galapoor already, or maybe another station?

"Jeevan." I shake him gently by the shoulder. "Jeevan, wake up."

He blinks. "What?"

"The train's just stopped but I don't know where we are."

The thud of footsteps on the ground outside the carriage sends me into a panic. "What if it's the police looking for two runaways?" My heart is pounding so hard I think it might explode.

Seconds later, a hand pulls the door open and we curl ourselves as small as possible behind our sacks, out of sight.

"Load them over here."

I make myself as invisible as I can. *Please don't find us.*

Light floods into the carriage and shines right where we're hiding, and I think we're going to be discovered, but the people outside carry on talking and laughing, loading more sacks into the train.

For a moment, I think we've made it—but then I hear

Jeevan breathing to stop a sneeze. I will him to smother it, but he can't and it comes out in a huge blast.

My heart speeds up as I hear sacks being dragged across the floor and the one right in front of us being lifted.

"What's this?" The man looks confused.

I pull Jeevan up by the arm and we both start to run but the man easily blocks our exit. My palms turn clammy. What will he do with us? "Don't tell the ticket collector," I plead.

He hesitates for a moment and backs out onto the platform, and for a second it looks like he's about to close the door. "Sorry." He shrugs.

A train guard scurries up behind him. "What's going on?" he asks.

"I was loading the cargo," he says. "Found these kids hiding behind the sacks."

"Stowaways?" asks the guard, his narrow eyes turning to slits as he catches sight of us. We get ready to run. "Hey!" he yells, grabbing me roughly by the arm before I can slip past. He pulls me out of the train.

My ankle twists as I land on the hard ground but I

don't shout out, even though the pain sears up my leg.

Jeevan jumps out of the carriage and lands next to me. "Are you okay?"

"Yes," I say, scrambling up.

"I wouldn't be surprised if you two boys have been thieving. What have you got in there?" He tries to prod his hand into my bag.

"We're not thieves," I say, snatching my bag away. "Get off me."

"Come on, Asha."

The doors slam shut as the whistle blows and the train snakes away from us, toward the snowy mountains of Galapoor, while we're left behind on the platform with the guard.

"Please let us go. We're not thieves," I say again.

He looks at us, eyes even more narrowed, but he must decide to believe me—or maybe we're just not worth the trouble. "Get out of here," he says, "before I call the police." He stands with his arms folded, watching as we walk away from the lonely station.

"What shall we do now?" asks Jeevan.

"I don't know," I say, trying hard not to cry, my ankle

throbbing with each step. The evening is strangely still, the eerie call of a single hunting owl piercing the silence.

"How far do you think it is to Galapoor?" asks Jeevan.

"Maybe it's not too far." My voice is small. "Let's look at your map. A boy in the market made me drop mine in a huge puddle before I even left Sonahaar, and anyway yours is way better."

"The sign at the station said 'Lahan,'" says Jeevan, cheering up a little.

After a moment's searching, I put my finger on the small town where we've been thrown off. "We're here." I can't bring myself to say it but we're miles away from Galapoor, from the mountains, and from Zandapur on the other side.

Jeevan looks at the map and then at me. "So we're not very close."

As we speak, dusk spreads its dark cloak around us and we know that nighttime with all its terrors will soon follow. "No," I say, wishing we could sprout wings to fly. "We're not very close at all."

CHAPTER
14

We trudge away from the station, along the rough, dirt-packed road, shivering against the cooling mountain air, our hopes of making it to Galapoor by nightfall in tatters.

Jeevan won't meet my gaze, keeping his eyes fixed to the ground. "I didn't mean to sneeze . . . I tried, but I couldn't hold it in."

"It's not your fault," I say. I'm annoyed at what happened, but I know we have to put it behind us.

He gives a deep sigh. "Papa will be back home by now and he'll have to tell my ma what I've done."

I've never spent a single night away from home and

imagine my empty bed opposite Rohan and Roopa's. I'm always the first to hear them if they wake in the night and I know they'll be missing me already.

"Let's send them a postcard when we get a chance. Then at least they'll know we're safe."

He shrugs his shoulders, like he's exasperated with himself and can't shake it off. I know he feels bad about us getting thrown off the train, but I don't want him to feel any worse. I swallow my disappointment. "We have to toughen up. We're bound to meet more people like that guard."

"That man had no right to treat us like thieves when he knows nothing about us," he says, swiping at a tall plant of chickweed growing along the side of the road.

"*We* know we're on an important journey," I say, hobbling alongside him. "Whatever he said doesn't matter."

As if someone is blowing out candles, the light is disappearing before our eyes. "Let's look for somewhere to sleep. We might find an old farm building or something." I spot a tall pistachio tree a little way off the road. "What about sleeping under there? It'll be just like those nights when we camped out late in the mango tree."

"Yeah . . . We can shelter right under the branches," says Jeevan. "And it'll keep the rain off as well."

We tramp across the muddy field toward the tree, its branches, laden with nuts, almost touching the ground.

"We'll be safe in here," I say, flopping down beside the canopy. "And look, we can even have a feast." I pick a handful of pale pistachios off the ground and begin to prize them open, laying the empty shells in patterns on the ground. I take a dry twig and dig it into the soil, strike one of the matches from my bag, and light it. "I missed not lighting the deeva tonight." I press my palms together. "Bless our journey, Lord Shiva, and watch over our families. Keep them safe until we return."

Jeevan puts his hands behind his head and lies down. "Not bad at all. Food, shelter, and prayers."

I let the makeshift deeva burn itself out. "I put eggs and a mango in my bag this morning, but let's save those for tomorrow and manage on the nuts for now."

"Really?" Jeevan looks disappointed.

"We have to be careful with supplies and there are loads of nuts. Even enough for you!"

I take out Papa's scarf, almost as big as a shawl, and

lay it on the hard ground. "Come here . . . It makes a great bed."

We lie in the shelter of the tree, darkness swooping down on us like a wide-winged bird. Stars begin to pierce the sky just like they do in Moormanali, but I can't believe that these are the same stars that shine on our grazing pastures and farm. I think of Ma, miles away, having to do all the jobs by herself, and I steel my heart to stop it from wandering back there.

"So, you thinking about home?" asks Jeevan.

"Yes."

"Me too."

I prop myself up on my elbow. "OK, Jeevan . . . here's the plan. Tomorrow we'll carry on walking toward Galapoor, go to the temple at Kasare, and before we know it we'll be in Zandapur. We'll find Papa and head straight back home and everyone will be amazed."

"And they'll be so proud of what we've done," says Jeevan excitedly. "We're not going to let this setback get us down!"

We eat our supper of soft green pistachios and watch the sky getting starrier.

"It's like someone's hurled deevay into the sky," I say.

"Well, you know that a star is just a luminous ball of gas, mostly hydrogen and helium, and it's only held together by its own gravity."

"Is that what Mr. Dhalia told you in physics?" I ask. "Has he ever been up in space, though? It's much nicer to think of them as deevay . . . Can you find Orion?" We love playing hunting stars back home and I want to cheer us both up with one of our games.

"There's his belt," he says, staring into the sky. "Have you found it yet?"

"Yes." I look up at the neat line of stars. "Can you see his bow?"

"Got it," he says. "And his little dog?"

"Down by his foot." I feel myself relaxing a little.

The sky flashes as stars shoot across the darkness, zipping over Orion's shoulders.

"That means we're going to be lucky," I say.

Jeevan smiles, shuffling into the canopy of the tree, and stretches. "Let's get some sleep."

In the far distance some creature gives a soulful bark and I imagine a wolf baring its teeth before the full moon. I crawl under the branches and shuffle closer to Jeevan.

"What's that?" I ask.

"It's only a dog," he says, yawning.

"Are you sure it's not something more dangerous? We're out in the wild now... And do you remember the stories of the half man, half beast they say haunts the high Himalayas?"

"I've told you before—they're just stories... The Musketeers sleep anywhere and aren't afraid of anything," says Jeevan.

The full moon rises like a huge silver paisa, shedding its pale light into the tree. It's six weeks to Divali and we'll have found Papa way before then, and he'll pay Ma's debt and write to Uncle Neel and tell him we're not coming to England after all.

"I'm on my way," I whisper, listening to the howling night sounds like hungry spirits on the wind. The warm metal of Nanijee's pendant presses against my skin and I clench my fingers around it.

CHAPTER

15

I wake up from a dream, confused to find myself curled into a frozen ball with Jeevan snoring next to me, and then I remember how we ended up here.

My body aches from lying on the hard ground and my neck is stiff, but I sit up in the darkness and peer out of the tree, rubbing my eyes. The first rays of sun crack out of the steely clouds and spool onto the distant snowy mountains.

We must get to Galapoor today, so we can get to Zandapur as soon as possible and find Papa.

I shake Jeevan. "Wake up. It's dawn already."

A little black-and-white bird flies into the tree and

begins scratching at the ground. I crumble a purple-streaked pistachio on my palm and hold it out. "You'll like this."

It takes a small beakful and flies off through the branches.

"Come on, sleepyhead!" I take the lamagaia feather and brush it across Jeevan's eyes.

"Where am I?" he asks, sitting up abruptly.

"We're on our journey, remember? The Two Musketeers?"

"Slow down, Asha," says Jeevan, yawning. "I need a minute or two to come around . . . Shall we have the mango?" He shoves his hand in my bag, finds the mango, and begins peeling it with the penknife.

"The sooner we get started, the sooner we'll find Papa."

He carries on peeling the fruit. "I'm sorry," he says.

"What for?"

"That I didn't come with you straightaway." He hands me a slice of mango. "You've hardly been out of Moormanali. It took real courage to come all by yourself."

"And I'm sorry too—you had good reasons for not coming. I wanted to say goodbye properly, I wanted to call you back and give you a hug, but I just couldn't."

I pull Nanijee's gold pendant from under the hoodie and stare at its teardrop shape. "It sounds strange," I say, letting myself trust Jeevan more now, knowing that he won't make fun of me like he used to—even if he isn't quite convinced. "As soon as Ma gave this to me, I knew I could do it. Whenever I hold it I feel something . . . like a force connecting me with my nanijee."

"I really want to believe you," he says, deep in thought.

We finish the rest of the mango in silence.

"Pass me the mango stone." I twist the banana leaf around it, tucking the end to make its own little plant pot, and scoop some dark red earth into it. I cradle it between my palms and close my eyes. "Grow, grow, sweet mango," I sing, "carried all the way from Moormanali, push out your greenest shoots for Papa to remind him of home."

I press the soil firmly and drip water onto it. "I'm

going to anoint it with the Holy Ganges when we get to the temple," I say, cocooning it in Papa's scarf and placing it in my bag.

We walk along a steep road fringed with tall deodar pines and wild rosebushes, which have shed their white petals and left behind fat orange hips. A tuneful whistling thrush, its deep blue feathers speckled with white, lands on a branch and looks at us.

The sun is almost overhead before we spot any signs for Galapoor, and then a truck comes blasting down the road, sounding its horn, shattering the peace, flicking a dusty trail of dirt and stones into my eyes.

"How long have we been walking?" I ask, slowing down. "I'm really thirsty."

"I don't know," says Jeevan, looking back the way we've come. "But I'm sure we'll come across a stream now that we're going higher."

I'm trying not to think about it, but my throat is parched and my ankle is starting to ache again.

"Look at that massive bird," says Jeevan in wonder, pointing down the road. "I think it's following us!"

I shade my eyes and spot the bird; it stays just ahead of us, stopping every time we do, and my heart gives a little skip. It's a lamagaia. "Do you believe the spirits of our ancestors live through animals, Jeevan?"

"Mmm ... I'm not sure ... it doesn't sound very likely."

I ignore his doubts. "I think it's true. I think this bird is keeping an eye on us." Could it be my nanijee's spirit?

It perches on a roadside rock and carries on watching us. I wave it farewell as we pass by and I catch sight of its dark eyes just before it takes off. "Come back soon, spirit bird!" I cry as it swoops over our heads.

I take out the feather I found the very first time I saw the bird and wish I still had my long braid to weave it into. Instead, I stroke it against my cheek before putting it back for safekeeping. Jeevan walks beside me, a slight frown on his face, as if he's trying to work out what he really believes.

We climb farther uphill on the road, which sweeps away toward lines of steep terraces planted with row after row of small, shiny tea plants. People are hunched over them with baskets on their backs, filled with bright green leaves.

The ankle I twisted yesterday is throbbing, sharp shooting pains crawling up my leg every time I take a step. I stop and rest against a post, turning away as more trucks loaded up with crates of fresh tea blast along the road.

"Do you think any of these drivers would give us a lift? I really need to rest my ankle."

Jeevan sticks his arm out. "Let's try. The next one might."

But not a single truck stops. I don't know how much farther I can walk and my ankle begins to howl more than ever. I collapse onto the edge of the road.

CHAPTER

16

Jeevan rushes to my side. "Are you OK?"

I lift my jeans and rub my swollen ankle. "It's really sore," I say, gritting my teeth. "But I'm sure I'll be fine."

He pulls me up. "Let's keep going, then."

Jeevan seems so full of energy, and he's right.

"Every step counts," he continues. "Come on, grab hold of my arm."

We shuffle along together, Jeevan dragging me with him each time I fall back. A long time passes before we hear another engine rumble.

"This one might stop." Jeevan sticks out his arm again, full of enthusiasm.

My heart gives a leap as the truck begins to slow down.

"We can say we're going to stay with our auntie in Galapoor," he says, grinning. "People will wonder why two kids are traveling alone."

The truck stops and a man with a thick curly mustache sticks his head out the window.

"Want a lift?"

Relief washes over me. "Yes," I shout, trying to get my voice heard over the roar of the truck.

The man swings the door open and we scramble up.

"Oooh," says the man, laughing. "With green eyes like yours you could be in the movies!"

I lower my gaze and look out the window, ignoring the man's comment . . . I need to blend in.

Dangling from the mirror is a picture of the black goddess Kali. She's surrounded by a fringe of silver tinsel, to bring the driver luck. On the dashboard is a photo of his family in a fluffy pink frame.

"Where are you two lads off to?" he asks.

"We're going to see our auntie. We lost our money and got kicked off the train. She lives just outside Galapoor on the road to Kasare," Jeevan says, squeezing my arm discreetly.

The driver nods and rams his foot on the accelerator. As the truck speeds off I look in the side mirror at the road behind us, the dirty gray fumes pumping against the blue sky as we shoot toward the town.

"I'm Krishen. Pleased to meet you," he says. "I'm not going as far as Galapoor . . . that OK?"

"Anywhere close is fine," says Jeevan.

I'm happy to let him do the talking. I don't want to draw any more attention to myself and even though I'm deepening my voice it might still make him suspicious.

Loud music with a heavy drumbeat and a strong rhythm blares inside the truck.

"Latest movie," says the driver, pausing from singing along badly. "You know, my cousin works in Bollywood, driving famous actors around. Last week he had Shah Rukh Khan in his car." He bangs the dashboard as if it's a drum and the picture of Kali bobs along as if she's in the movie as well. I nudge Jeevan's foot, and we both giggle.

We climb even higher, leaving the terraces behind, the road now lined with wild fruit trees, stretching out against the horizon. Every now and then we pass small buildings at the roadside with handwritten signs for chai and coconut juice, pakoray and hot potato dhosay. The truck hugs the tight bends upward, teetering against the crumbling edge of road, scaling the mountain, farther into the high Himalayas.

We stop suddenly and I wake with a dry mouth and a tongue that won't move to ask where we are.

"First stop, dhabba stall," says Krishen. "Galapoor's not far now."

"We haven't got much money," I say, trying not to think about the lovely food they'll have at the stall.

"He owes me a favor, this dhabba man. Forget the money this time, OK?"

Jeevan licks his lips, looking famished. "Thanks," he shouts, opening the door and jumping onto the ground.

I notice that the stall has a rack of cards with stamps already on them. "Let's send a postcard home."

"It'll be good to let them know that at least we're safe," says Jeevan.

"And by the time they get it, we'll be miles away. I think we can afford one."

I find my purse, give the stallholder a coin for the card, and borrow his pen. I'm so hot I pull off my hoodie, wrap it around my waist, and sit on a rock to begin writing.

> Dear Ma, Rohan, and Roopa,
> I hope you are managing the chores
> without me.
> Jeevan and I are looking after each other.
> We are closer to finding Papa. We will be
> back as soon as we can.
> Love, Asha
> XXX

I hand the card to Jeevan so he can write his message.

"There's a postbox here," he says, finishing the card off with a row of kisses and pushing it through the slot.

"Best pakoray this side of Galapoor," says a small, wiry boy working at the dhabba stall. He stands on a box so he can reach the stove. He looks directly at us, frowns, then scoops up fresh pakora batter and plops it into the wide frying pan, making the oil crackle. Steam whooshes up as the pakoray turn a mouthwatering golden color and he adds them to the heaps already piled high on a brass tray.

"I've been told to give you some for free," says the boy, handing us a bag brimming with food. "How come you two are traveling by yourselves anyway?" The boy steps closer and even though I'm looking down at the ground, he pushes his face right into mine and eyes Jeevan suspiciously.

I turn my back to him and bite into a crunchy pakora.

"Me and my brother are going to meet our auntie," says Jeevan.

"That's a funny brother," the boy says. "*Pretty, isn't he?*"

Jeevan suddenly turns very red—the boy's guessed *I'm* not a boy at all, but neither of us knows what to say.

Jeevan stands between the boy and me.

"What's wrong with you?" he says to Jeevan. "I bet you like her, don't you?"

I walk a few paces back, feeling my cheeks turning more crimson than Jeevan's.

Anger puffs out of Jeevan like hot steam as he rushes right up to the boy and pushes him hard. "Don't talk about her."

The boy turns his fists into tight balls. "I'll fight you if you want!" He pushes Jeevan back.

"Hey!" Jeevan spins around, getting ready to throw a punch, but the boy gets there first, swinging his fist into Jeevan's chin and knocking him to the ground. The boy crouches over him and draws back his fist again.

"Get off him!" I cry, pushing the boy hard. "He's fought off bigger men than you can imagine! Now, get out of our way and leave us alone." I turn my back on him, offer Jeevan my hand, and help him up.

"What an idiot," says Jeevan, brushing off the dust.

The boy is simmering with rage. "I know where I've seen you before—they put out a call for you this morning, on the local TV news. They said you were runaways. Not such an idiot now, am I?" He's already pulling a phone from his pocket.

I clasp my hands to my mouth. "Oh no!" I cry, my insides full of fireworks. "We have to go before he calls the police." I grab Jeevan's arm and begin to pull him away. "We can't go home yet!"

Krishen and the dhabba man walk over from the other side of the stall.

"Hey," snaps the stallholder, slapping the boy on the back of the head. "Do I pay you to fight with my customers?"

The boy scowls and returns to his place by the hot oil.

"Kids!" says Krishen, climbing back into his truck. "No more getting into trouble, eh?" He laughs. "That road will take you toward Galapoor."

"Thanks for the food and the lift," says Jeevan. We wave him off as the truck pulls away.

A look of worry appears in Jeevan's eyes as we set off in the opposite direction.

We walk off-road to avoid other travelers, but try to stay as close to the road as we can to keep our bearings. We're constantly looking over our shoulders. The path dips and bends, sometimes coming near to the road and at other times taking us away from where we want to go.

"It's getting darker now," I say. "I think we could walk along the edge of the road without being recognized."

We stumble down the gritty bank and begin walking along the tarmac in single file.

Suddenly we're caught in the glare of icy-white headlights, and a screech of brakes sends fear spiraling through me. I scrunch my eyes and make out the ghostly silhouette of a police car.

"Asha, run!"

We scramble back up the steep bank, kicking rocks behind us.

"Wait!" one of the police officers shouts.

I can hear heavy breathing as the men struggle to keep up.

We don't stop until we reach a clump of trees way above the road.

"Quick," cries Jeevan. "Up there."

I grasp the branch, my hands shaking, and hoist myself into the pine tree, Jeevan scrambling up behind.

"Where are you?" a distant voice calls out of the darkness, followed by a faint flashlight beam. "Come down. You're not in trouble. Your parents are worried."

The beam gets brighter and my heart pumps harder as it comes to a stop right under the tree.

I grip the branch even tighter.

Jeevan takes hold of my other hand, but he daren't speak. My heart is thumping furiously, fear and confusion filling my thoughts. Part of me wants to climb down, to go home to safety. But I know I have to finish this journey I've started, or there won't be a home for me there anymore.

Eventually the flashlight beam passes. We listen to the footsteps fading, an engine starting up again somewhere nearby. Finally we risk climbing down from the tree.

We continue along on lonely mountain tracks,

crossing rivers swollen with rain, sleeping rough wherever we can with hardly anything to eat but wild fruit. We've added days to our journey trying to stay hidden—but there's no doubt in my mind: We mustn't get caught.

CHAPTER

17

Our progress to Kasare is painfully slow. For the next few days we pick our way along rough, half-made paths, trying to keep the road in sight as much as possible. We shelter under trees and scavenge what food we can from villages and fields, and refill our water bottles at every opportunity.

My stomach feels like it has a huge hole in it that will never be full again and all I can think of is how fantastic it would be to have a whole pile of Ma's fresh naan that puff out steam when you break into them, stuffed with milky paneer, instead of eating only the tiny berries we've found.

"I'm starving. Have you got anything else to eat in your bag?" asks Jeevan, stopping by a tree, his cheekbones making sharp hollows in his face.

"If only." I stop beside him, my legs shaky. "There aren't even any chickens about. At least around Galapoor we could steal a few eggs—I know they were disgusting raw but they kept us going."

"Yeah . . . but that was ages ago." He twists to face me and the sudden shock of seeing the way his collarbone juts from his T-shirt makes me wish I had something to give him.

"Just think, when we get to the temple we can have a pilgrim's meal."

"*When* we get to the temple . . . That's what you keep saying!"

"It's not *my* fault . . . I'm hungry too, you know!"

As each night falls and the moon gets smaller, it reminds me that I don't have much time left to find Papa—it's only five weeks until Divali, until Ma gives up on our family and decides to go.

Even though I've stuffed leaves into my shoes, my blisters have turned into bloodied scabs and rub even more. Sharp stones push through the worn soles, stabbing at my feet, and my swollen ankle is covered in a multicolored bruise.

"We've already been traveling a whole week," I say, dragging myself along the worn path that leads to the temple at Kasare and then on to Zandapur. "Why is it taking so long?"

"I've had enough," says Jeevan, breathing quickly, giving a noisy cough.

"We have to keep moving. The police won't have given up—they'll be looking for us even up here."

"Look," says Jeevan. "The weather's changing."

I stare into the sky, pale and laden with snow, and feel so tiny against the towering mountains ahead, their never-ending steep slopes stretching toward the clouds like stalagmites.

"I can't believe how cold it is," I say, puffing hot breath into my hands and pulling at my sleeves. "Look how the countryside's changing too. Even the grass is hurting my feet, it's so dry and coarse."

"I need to rest," says Jeevan. "I'm worn out. Let's stop a minute and look at the map."

We sit together on the grass and he pulls it from his bag, spreading it out on the ground. "I think this is where we are now." He puts his finger just below Kasare.

"Well, do you know, or do you just think?" My question sounds more spiky than I mean it to.

"I'm doing my best to navigate. You can look at the map as well, you know."

I try to control myself and make a point of speaking more gently this time. "I'm sorry . . . We're both tired. Is that the village we passed earlier this morning?"

"Yes," he says, examining the map more carefully. "I'm sure it is."

"It doesn't look like there are any more villages between here and Kasare." I trace our journey so far. "And look, the path goes through that huge forest . . . and Kasare and Zandapur are beyond that."

"There will still be the odd house—families who keep goats, that sort of thing."

I peel the sneakers off my feet and touch the mess of bloodied, raw blisters, wincing as I squeeze them back in. "You're right." I clamp my teeth hard to stop myself from crying. "I'm sure we'll find shelter if the weather gets bad. Shall we get going? If I sit still for any longer my feet will give up."

I limp along, following the path as it gets steeper and steeper. We're so incredibly high it makes my head spin when I glance back at the villages we've passed, like tiny specks now. In the distance I can see a lake, so far away but still shimmering like a vast mirror, bordered by the lush green grass of the lower slopes. If I squint I can just make out a fishing boat with a tiny sail, gliding slowly across the water as if it's being pulled by magic.

I force myself forward, feeling my muscles stretched taut with each new step. I round a corner in the path and my eyes light up.

"Look! Jeevan." A string of prayer flags flutters in the cold breeze, like red flames sent to keep us warm. "Come on . . . That means we're going in the right direction."

Jeevan is looking really pale. "I'm so tired," he says, leaning against a wild fig tree.

I grab his arm and pull him along. "We can play our favorite game." Perhaps this will take our minds off the walking. "What would you most like to eat?"

"A big plate of chicken cooked in the tandoor," he says breathlessly. "With a squeeze of fresh lime juice all over it."

"Do you remember when we helped Papa dig a fire pit on the grazing grounds and we cooked a chicken together and then camped out?"

"Yeah... It was... great... W–what about you?" wheezes Jeevan, slowing down again.

"Three of Ma's soft potato parathay, washed down with a big glass of mango lassi, then maybe one or two sweet jelaybia." My stomach gives a hollow growl.

"I thought you wanted to get to Zandapur as soon as you could," says Jeevan out of the blue. "Maybe we should have gone straight there, on the road." He stops walking and sits on a log to rest. "We could have been there by now."

"*What* is wrong with you? You know exactly why. The police are hunting for us... *all over the roads*!" I kick loose rocks down the path. "You're being so difficult!" I swivel around and walk ahead, leaving him behind. When I turn to look for him he's hardly moved at all.

"Why don't you just go back to the last village?" I shout. "I can go on by myself."

"Maybe I will." His words catch hold of the breeze and follow me up the path.

Guilt winds itself around me and I wait while he catches up. He doesn't look well at all. "My legs are aching," he says, and my temper flares again.

"So are mine. It's just the walking—you saw my feet! We've got to keep going, Jeevan!" Why does he keep arguing? I've had enough now. "I'm tired as well but *I'm* not complaining." I fling this last sentence at him. "Walk as slowly as you want. I'm going." I can see the forest ahead and hobble on without looking back.

When I get there I still don't wait but limp down a path that leads into a gloomy thicket of tall pines and find myself engulfed in darkness. Silent shadows and a resinous scent hang heavy in the air, but I go farther into the trees, still not stopping or looking back for Jeevan.

A twig cracks beneath my foot, the sound sending strange-sounding birds squawking through the forest.

And that's when I come to my senses; what am

I thinking? I turn and look back along the path toward the entrance to the forest, but can't see Jeevan anywhere.

Without the sun to warm me, the cold is seeping into my bones, and even though my feet are smarting, I run toward the light, back the way I've come, to find him.

I stand at the tree line and see him walking slowly, almost shuffling along. I cup my hands to my mouth. "Jee-van."

He waves to me from a distance but as he gets closer, I notice how bright his cheeks are.

"Let's not fight," I say when he finally reaches me. "We have to stick together . . . Let's look at the map again. We don't want to get lost." I shove my hand into his bag and try to grasp it but my fingers come out empty. "Jeevan, are you sure you put it back last time you looked?"

"*Yes, Asha,* I'm sure I did . . . What about *you? You lost yours in a puddle even before we started the journey!*"

I empty the whole bag onto the ground, then rummage through my own. "I can't find it anywhere. One of us has left it somewhere and it's probably blown away. Now we'll have no way of knowing where we're going."

My stomach stabs with panic. How are we going to get to Papa on time *now*?

Jeevan looks at the sky. "Well, we know we're heading north . . . and the sun is over there . . ." He lowers his head. "We have to go through the forest, that's for sure. I remember it from the map. We'll carry on and then when it gets dark I'll use the stars to make sure we're still going north."

I tell myself to stop panicking—Jeevan can read the stars as easily as storybooks; of course we won't get lost.

We don't speak, just continue into the forest, keeping to the pine needle–covered tracks until we're swallowed by a shadow of the darkest green.

CHAPTER

18

We've been walking through the forest for a long time, the shady branches making everything gloomy. I jump at each rustle of the pine trees, each snap of a twig, frightened that some predator is stalking us. Jeevan begins coughing and I'm worried that he really *is* ill.

I thread my arm through his as each silent step takes us even deeper into the forest. I stare through the branches at the patches of whitening sky. "Let's find somewhere to shelter. It's getting colder and the weather's changing so suddenly."

After a few more minutes my misty breath spirals

into the cold air and something wet lands on my nose, making me look up. "It's snowing." I remember Chitragupta's words about staying together in the high Himalayas and I feel sick and full of anger at myself for leaving Jeevan behind earlier.

He sits down on the freezing forest floor. "Asha, I can't go on. I mean it." His eyes are bloodshot.

I touch Jeevan's blazing forehead and the guilt twists into me like a burning knife. "We'll find some shelter, Jeevan, I promise." After everything we said about looking after each other, I can't believe I didn't notice sooner that he wasn't well.

He closes his eyes. "I'll be OK." His voice is weak and shaky.

"I'm so sorry for leaving you back there. Can you forgive me?" He doesn't reply. The icy snowflakes are beginning to settle on the ground. "We must find a shepherd's hut or something, there has to be one up here.

"Hold on to me, Jeevan," I continue, hooking his arm around my waist. "We'll find somewhere to sleep the night and . . . and you'll feel better in the morning."

We struggle through the trees, branches scraping our skin.

Panic stabs at my chest but I won't give in to it. If anything happens to Jeevan it will be all my fault. I have to be even stronger now. I take a deep icy breath and grip him more tightly, using all my strength to keep him from falling.

We move slowly and the snow begins to fall in flurries, as if someone's shaking a feather pillow in the air. Large white flakes drift down through the trees, coating everything, including the path, in a dense layer of freezing snow. I squint ahead at the disappearing track, desperate for a sign of shelter, but there's nothing, only trees.

Even though he's lost weight, Jeevan is still taller and heavier than I can manage and I have to get him to sit down on the cold ground each time I need a rest.

Feeling his forehead again, he's much hotter than before and his cheeks are brighter too. He closes his eyes again and this time falls onto his back.

"Jeevan . . . Jeevan!" I scream. "Can you hear me?"

"Yes," he says faintly.

Tears stream down my face; I won't let him die like his brother. "You're going to get better, OK?"

But he doesn't answer.

The air is bitter. I get Papa's scarf out of my bag, not worrying about the mango stone it's protecting, and wrap it around his shoulders to keep him warm. I try to lift him off the ground, but I can't do it.

I pull and pull until with one final heave that leaves me gasping for air, he stands up.

"We have to keep going, Jeevan," I say, fighting back my sobs. His body is heavy against my shoulder. I grip my pendant, begging it to give me courage.

We slip along together, taking small steps, zigzagging this way and that, scouring the trees for a hut to protect him from the snow.

I look around in desperation. What can I do? His breath sounds more and more labored and raspy... The only thing I can think of is to build a shelter myself.

There's a huge boulder and mounds of thick fallen branches on the ground. I prop him up against a fallen log and get to work, dragging long heavy branches through the pine needles and snow and balancing them close together against the rock.

The snow is flying down, covering Jeevan in frozen flakes, and the longer it takes me to build the shelter, the colder he's getting—I must move faster.

"I'm making a tree den, Jeevan." I keep talking so he'll stay awake. "Just like the ones we make back home."

I collect smaller branches with pine needles still on them and make a second layer to keep the wind from getting through. Splinters pinch my skin and my muscles ache from all the walking and lifting, but I carry on building until it's finished and my breath bursts out in ragged gasps.

"Jeevan . . . Can you walk a little?"

He's still awake but keeps closing his eyes and drifting away. I help him stand up and lead him into the pine-covered shelter, pulling the scarf more tightly around him.

I sit next to him, allowing myself a moment of satisfaction, but I can't rest until I've built a fire to keep the wild animals away.

On cold winter evenings, on the grazing grounds, Papa and I used to build fires together, so I know exactly how to do it.

"Hurry, hurry," I whisper to myself. The soil on the forest floor is soft and comes away easily as I dig into the ground with a pointed stick, hollowing out a pit. I crouch down and scrape at the earth, flicking it everywhere until the deep hole is ready.

"I'm building a fire, Jeevan," I say, slipping on the snow. I pull my hood closer to my face, but the wind forces it back, blowing icy flakes into my eyes.

I fish through my bag, find the penknife, and use it to strip bark off a tree for kindling, which I pile up in the fire pit, ready to light.

I layer the fire just like Papa showed me and move my numb hands slowly, trapping a match between my thumb and forefinger. I strike it against the box, but it tumbles to the wet ground.

I clench my jaw to fight back the tears as more snow begins to pile up against the shelter. Using all my concentration, I strike the match again. It sparks and I nudge the yellow flame toward the fine strips of kindling. It crackles straightaway, but the kindling burns in a second, then dies out.

I check on Jeevan inside the shelter, tell myself to stay calm, and go through each step once more. This time it works. I've done it. It's a small fire, but the bark is alight. I gather smaller sticks and edge them toward the flame, which grows stronger. The glowing logs sizzle and spit as the storm blows even more fiercely.

I collect the drier branches from under the trees and pile them onto the fire, saving some in the shelter so we can have dry wood for the morning.

Inside, Jeevan coughs and mumbles and the snow keeps falling, floating through the trees, turning everything ghostly white.

I hope the fire is big enough to keep the tigers and leopards away through the night.

I take a glowing stick from the fire, look into the opening of the shelter at Jeevan with his eyes closed tight, and imagine that it's incense. I circle him with the smoking ember and say a prayer.

I throw the stick back in the fire, take Jeevan's hand, and hold it tight.

If only you'd stayed at home like you planned, you would have been safe.

"I'm here," I whisper, tears sliding down my face. "You're just tired, that's all, you'll be fine in the morning..."

And then I say another prayer, in silence this time.

Please get better... Please, Lord Shiva, don't let him die.

CHAPTER
19

All through the long fear-filled night, I listen to the wind whistling through the branches of the shelter, petrified that Jeevan is getting worse, or that the fire will go out. I imagine snow leopards waiting in the darkness, ready to pounce and devour us.

"Ma!" calls Jeevan, coughing. "Are you all right, Ma? I'm sorry."

I leap to feel his forehead. It's hotter than yesterday and even now, in the first light of dawn, his cheeks are burning.

"Jeevan?" I whisper softly, stroking his hair, like I know his ma would.

He's lost in his own deep cavern of fever and haunted dreams and doesn't answer.

"Jeevan," I try again.

His laugh is high and strange sounding. "The tigers," he says, gasping. "My papa said be careful of the tigers."

He's not making any sense, but I know it's the fever speaking. Once, when I was ill, Ma told me I said odd things in the night. She laid a fresh cotton sheet on my bed, dampened my forehead with a cool cloth, and stayed with me until I was better.

I have to get this scarf off, but it's so tightly wound around him that I can't. He needs to stay cool—I should have done this last night. I grip it tightly, tugging it free, and hurl it aside. "I'm so sorry. I promise I'll look after you better."

I look out into the smoky-gray dawn, the wind whirling loose pine needles from the trees in spirals to the ground. I'm grateful that at least it's stopped snowing, and even though the fire is smaller, it's still glowing.

There's no food left in the bag, only the water we collected yesterday, and I know if I want to save Jeevan,

I have to find help. But without a map to guide me, how will I find my way? Jeevan is the star reader.

I prop him up and put a bottle of water to his lips. "Jeevan? Try to drink this."

He sips with his eyes still closed and I lay him down again, dampening the edge of the scarf, dabbing his forehead with cold water. I don't want to leave him in case the fire goes out and his human scent calls animals from miles away, but if I don't go, he might die. Fever claimed his brother and now might be coming for him, and guilt stabs me again and again.

Outside, everything is hushed and veiled in white. I hear something move far up in the trees and raise my head to see what it is. A lump of snow falls to the ground by my foot and a loud clucking sound makes me jump.

The spirit bird! Its wing tips are outstretched as it flies down through the branches and lands on top of the shelter.

My heart pounds with amazement and gratitude. "Have you come to help?" I begin to feel braver and more certain that it must be Nanijee, because why else would I sense that rhythm again, the one that feels like it's connecting me to my ancestors, making me feel less alone in this forest wilderness?.

I stand on a log and stretch my fingers toward it like the last time, but now I really want to feel its feathers, to see whether the touch reminds me of my nanijee's hand. It stays still for a moment, bending its head toward me, but hops away as I try to stroke its wing. "Dearest Nanijee," I whisper. "It has to be you . . . Doesn't it?"

I jump to the ground and it sits watching while I bring the dry wood out of the shelter, piling the branches upright all around the glowing embers of the fire and pushing kindling into the gaps to get it going. I then stack all the wood on the fire so it's as high as I can make it, the dry wood crackling, shooting fiery sparks into the air and making my face tingle with heat. At last, I warm my frozen hands, raw and scratched from carrying the branches, and pause.

All this time the spirit bird stays on the shelter, keeping its eyes firmly fixed on me as I prepare to leave.

What did Jeevan say last time we looked at the map?

Something about the closest village, but I can't remember where he said it was . . . back the way we came or the other way? If I make a mistake, Jeevan could be the one paying the price . . . with his life.

I swallow the lump in my throat, fight back the tears that are sneaking out, and think of the warrior goddess Durga.

I kneel at the entrance to the shelter, touch Jeevan's cheek for the final time, and listen to his rattled breath heave in and out. "I won't leave you for long, I promise. I'll be back before the fire dies out."

The spirit bird calls again.

"Are you telling me to go? But how will I find my way back? The forest is vast, and without the map it all looks the same." My hand brushes the cotton bag I brought from home and I get an idea: I'll use the knife to cut it into strips and tie them to branches as I pass.

I lay my precious belongings to one side, pick up Jeevan's knife, and begin cutting the bag, counting the strips as I go. It makes forty altogether, and I stuff them into my pockets.

I take one last look at Jeevan, his breath rushing in

and out, his cheeks blazing, and my voice wavers. "I'll be back as soon as I can."

The spirit bird remains poised on the shelter, ruffles its coppery wings, turns its head, and blinks at me.

"Bless my journey and keep Jeevan safe." I press my hands together. "Guard him for me."

CHAPTER
20

Everything is deathly quiet as I creep away into the blanketed dawn, along the snowy path. I curl my numb fingers around one of the strips in my pocket and pull it out. I stretch up to a branch and tie it in a double knot before hurrying on.

I peer up into the sky, still semidark with the pin-prick lights of stars shining through. With Jeevan by my side it would be easy to know the right star to follow. He always said the North Star was the one to navigate by—it's the one that never moves. And if Jeevan can do it, so can I! His life depends on it. At the next clearing I look up and choose the stillest star, keep it ahead of me just like he would, and move forward.

Blood pumps in my ears as I search through the icy mist. Pale fingers of early sunlight cast long spiky shadows in the trees. What if the man-beast stories are real? I think of Nanijee, swallow my fears, feel my courage rise, and quicken my pace to find help for Jeevan, tying the strips as I go.

I keep walking through the shadowy forest, my eyes clamped firmly on the fading star, flashing furtive glances over my shoulder as invisible demons pierce their eyes into my back, until I'm tired and hungry and my legs are close to buckling beneath me.

I flop to the ground and rest against a tree, exhausted. I raise myself onto my elbows but can't get to my feet again.

Asha, you can't stay there. Remember my words when you fell from the mango tree and lay in a bundle by the base of the trunk, refusing to get up? I cradled you, dabbed your knees with a clean cloth, and together we walked back to the house. I fed you milky kheer between your sobs and told you the pain would soon be forgotten, but maybe the scars would stay to remind you to be strong when it happens again.

Go on, little Ashi, go on.

I push away from the tree. The final length of fabric is ready in my pocket, and I feel the rhythm of the pendant egging me on, the wild wind calling my name: *Aaaa . . . sha!*

I tug at the fabric and think of Jeevan, overcome by his fits of fever, and stagger through the craggy trees as rays of morning light creep through their branches. My heart is waking up, rapping at my ribs.

When the trees start to thin at long last as weak sunlight smudges the sky behind, I grasp the last tie with my frozen fingers and hook the fabric clumsily, lifting it slowly from my pocket, twisting it onto a branch in an awkward knot.

Aching deep into my bones, I drag myself through the final stretch of forest onto a wide plateau where coarse grasses stand to attention like ghostly snow-covered soldiers. And now that the sun has risen, I'm sure I'll find my way back.

The memory of Jeevan's face, fever stretched and

blazing, spurs me on, giving me the strength to keep tramping forward—past trees, through tall, grassy meadows, hardly stopping to rest until the sun is almost overhead, searching for a house, a goat, anything.

I cup my hands in an icy stream that springs out of a cluster of rocks and take a long, thirst-quenching drink.

I splutter the water out . . . It's faint at first, but I can hear the sound of goats bleating. I knew there would be farms out here! My heart gives a little skip—if there are goats there'll be someone looking after them! I squint against the sun but don't see anyone.

I begin running in the direction of the bleating and, putting my hands to my mouth, I call out, "Hey . . . Anybody there?" My voice is a lonely cry echoing across the wide-open land. "Anybody?" I repeat.

But there are only the bleating goats. I run toward them, slowing as I get closer, and whistle, trying to entice one toward me. I grab at a clump of bleached grass and hold the offering in the palm of my hand. "Come on . . . over here."

A curious black-and-white one sidles up, nosing its way toward my outstretched hand. "That's it . . . I'm not going to harm you." As soon as it begins to nibble at the grass, I hook my arm around the struggling creature and capture it. Its milk will be more than enough to make Jeevan better.

I fling off my hoodie and twist the arm around the goat's neck and tightly knot it. "Shhh . . ." I say, full of hope, turning back in the direction I've come from.

I hurry onward, pulling the goat with me back across the uneven ground, passing through clumps of trees and meadows full of grasses taller than my waist. I struggle up steep hills and cross trickling streams until the sun turns crimson and begins to lower in the sky.

The journey has taken all day and I feel my heart speed up as I think of what might have happened while I've been gone.

I'm coming, Jeevan, keep strong. I'm on my way.

I'm worn out but I wipe the hot sweat from my forehead and continue toward the forest and, at long last, reach its welcoming green edge.

I cast a glance behind me and enter the darkening

canopy of leaves, tugging the goat urgently. I begin scanning the branches for the first length of fabric that marks my way back to Jeevan.

Low-hanging branches scratch my cheeks as I hunt frantically for the first tie, but the rippling leaves cast confusing shadows and I can't see it anywhere.

I rest a moment, tired and frustrated, with the bewildered goat beside me. Then I continue combing the branches for the swirl of red fabric I tied this morning. And finally, I spot it, gently waving in the breeze.

"Hey . . . Hey, you!" I jump. "What do you think you're doing, stealing my goat?"

A dog bounds up, snarling and barking ferociously. Behind it is a boy a couple of years older than me, wearing a wide-brimmed felt hat and leading a horse.

"I wasn't stealing it." I stand as still as I can while the dog keeps barking, nipping and tearing the edge of my sleeve.

The boy steps in closer. "Well, it looks like stealing to me. I've been trailing you." He speaks in a strange dialect and I have to concentrate hard to understand him.

"My friend is very ill. He's got a fever. I had to leave him alone in the forest to find something to help him . . . Now, will you *please* call your dog off?"

The boy whistles and the dog releases its grip.

"Your friend? I don't understand . . . your accent." He takes off his hat, revealing wavy shoulder-length hair. "You're not from here, are you?"

I speak more slowly this time, my voice thick with panic. "No . . . but my friend, he is sick. I found your goat and I was going to give him some milk to make him better . . . We've been walking a long way without proper food . . . I would have brought it back. *Please*. I need your help."

The boy looks at me closely like he's trying to work me out.

I hold my head high. "I sacrificed my hair in return for blessings from the Gods . . . my name's Asha."

"I'm Nahul," he replies.

"We're on our way to Kasare . . . to the temple."

"My ma went there once," he says. "My baby sister was very ill, so she took offerings to the Daughter of the Mountain, to the source of the Ganges."

"That's what we're going to do . . . for my papa." I move closer to him. "The place I left him isn't far from here . . . Could I please give Jeevan some milk and then you can take your goat home?"

"I'm not sure. My family will be worried." He nods toward the setting sun. "And it'll be dark soon." He pulls his rifle across his chest.

I plead with him. "What if he got so weak that he couldn't survive the fever . . . or what if he's been attacked?" I wipe my cheeks.

Nahul stares into the gloom beyond the trees and then back along the path out of the forest, deciding what to do.

"I beg you." There's a long pause.

"OK," he says, still sounding unsure. "I'll come with you . . . but we must hurry."

He ties the goat with a long piece of rope and secures it to the horse's bridle, then holds the horse steady while I slot my foot into the stirrup and hoist myself up. "Thank you."

"Remember to duck under the low branches," he says, climbing up behind me and setting off.

Deep-throated animal howls haunt the strengthening wind as we journey on.

"What's that?"

"It sounds like a pack of wolves," he says, turning his head. "M-maybe they're missing one and are mourning their loss."

A ball of fear tightens as I think of Jeevan alone. "Can we go more quickly?"

As we trot along, hooves thudding against the ground, the howls sounding closer than ever, he twists the horse in the direction of the red ties, and each time I spot one my heart gives a leap.

I close my eyes and say a prayer for Jeevan, feeling for my pendant, gripping it tightly. "Be safe, Jeevan . . . Nanijee, keep him safe."

We keep riding through the forest until we're on the final slippery paths with rows of pines that I recognize. The horse tosses its head, suddenly skittish, but the forest is eerily quiet.

"Jeevan!" I cry out, fear whipping through my blood as we draw closer. "It's me . . . I'm back."

Nahul pulls on the reins to control the horse, bringing

it to a standstill near the edge of the clearing, stroking its neck soothingly. We dismount, but once we're out of the saddle the horse whinnies and rears, yanking the goat with it, as if it senses something we don't, as if it's trying to run away. My heart lurches in fear.

"Steady, boy . . . steady." Nahul holds on to the reins while I scramble toward the shelter. Something is wrong.

And as soon as I burst into the clearing I see it. Panic shoots through me like a bolt of electricity and I scream a high-pitched, sharp cry from the depths of my soul.

There's a tiger, prowling in front of the smoking fire, its amber-striped skin flashing golden in the setting sun, blood staining the corner of its mouth.

CHAPTER

21

The snow beneath the tiger's paws is speckled red. "Jeevan!" I cry, my breathing out of control. I lunge toward the fire and grab a smoldering log, the end in my hand not quite alight.

"Asha, move away!"

Nahul is behind me; from the corner of my eye I catch the glint of his rifle.

"No!" I cry out. "What if you hit Jeevan?" The tiger is standing right by the shelter where he's sleeping, hopefully alive—but defenseless.

I inch forward, and the glow from the fire lights up the tiger, its heavy shoulders taut with each slow step it takes toward the entrance of the shelter. It bows its head slightly and meets my gaze with its green eyes. The burning log trembles in my hand, and I remember the tigers in my vision at Chitragupta's house, the way they danced in the flames, circling me.

"What are you doing?" shouts Nahul from behind me. "Move away from it. I'm going to fire."

But I don't move; I stay facing the tiger as if I'm in a trance, our eyes locked.

The deafening shot echoes through the air above our heads, leaving the acrid smell of burnt powder, smoky and sharp. The shot lodges in a trunk at the other side of the clearing.

Nahul aimed high on purpose—a warning shot. The tiger throws its head back, opens its jaws, and gives a huge growl before disappearing into the forest.

I rush into the shelter on my hands and knees, panic coursing through me, afraid of what I'm about to find. "J-Jeevan?"

But there's no reply, only the moaning of the wind and the creaking trees.

He's lying just as I left him, eyes closed, his breath heaving in and out. Alive!

I wrap my arms around him, lay my head on his chest, and blink my tears away. "Thank you," I say, although I'm not sure who I'm speaking to. "I'm here," I whisper.

"Asha . . . Asha . . . Are you OK?" Nahul is outside, breathing heavily. "Look what I found on the other side." I leave Jeevan for a moment and follow Nahul around the back of the shelter.

Spread out on the ground lies the blood-smeared body of a wolf. I clench my stomach and turn away.

"It must have been the tiger," says Nahul. "Is your friend OK?"

I'm in a daze, still trying to work out what happened. "Y-yes . . . h-he hasn't been harmed."

"That's a miracle." Nahul's voice is full of awe. "The tiger protected your friend, Asha."

"I have to get him to safety . . . Will you help?"

"Of course."

I return to Jeevan. "Wake up," I say softly. "Wake up . . . please." His breathing is shallow and raspy, and when I shake him, he stays still, his eyelids fluttering. Is he better or worse than when I left him?

He stirs slightly and behind his eyes there's a flicker of movement. My heart lifts.

"Jeevan . . . it's me, Asha."

"I'll milk the goat," says Nahul, shifting away from the fire. "It's good, easy food . . . Grandmother would say it was in my karma to find you and that I should bring you home."

I lay more wood on the embers, blowing to get the fire started again, before going back inside to Jeevan.

After a minute or two, Nahul hands me his goatskin water carrier. "Here's the milk. Make sure you drink some as well. I'll get the horse ready."

"Thank you, Nahul." Sliding my arm around Jeevan's back, I prop him up and carefully tip the warm, fresh milk into his mouth.

He opens his eyes and splutters. "Asha?" he says faintly.

"Yes. It's me . . . Sip some more."

He takes a small gulp of milk and lets out a deep sigh. I give him another sip.

"Jeevan, we have to leave . . . You're not well and it's dangerous here."

Nahul comes back to the entrance. "Let's go—my family will be waiting for me. You're impressive—the shelter and the fire—you've probably saved your friend's life. *And* faced up to a tiger."

I feel myself swell with pride and take a long drink of milk before packing everything into Papa's scarf and tying a strong knot.

Jeevan sways as I lead him out of the shelter, and together Nahul and I struggle to get him onto the horse. Once we're ready we ride away through the forest, toward Nahul's house.

When we finally see the outline of the farmhouse, lit with pale lanterns, I pull my arms tighter around Jeevan, wondering what Nahul's family will say when he brings two complete strangers into their home. I feel more tired than ever, dark spots crowding the sides of my vision, my fingertips tingling.

Nahul slows the horse. "I'm back," he shouts. "And I've found a boy and a girl in the forest!" We come to a standstill and he jumps down.

Nahul helps us off the horse and I hold on to Jeevan to stop him from toppling over—even though I'm feeling shaky myself.

A group of people rush out of the house and stand in a confused semicircle surrounding us. I feel my stomach flip a somersault.

"Thank the stars you're back," says a tall woman who must be Nahul's ma. "We've been waiting and waiting . . . so worried."

"Who are they?" asks an older man gruffly.

"I am Asha. I'm from Moormanali in the foothills," I say with pride. "This is my friend Jeevan. We're on a journey to find my papa in Zandapur, and we're going to stop at Kasare on our way to make a pilgrimage." I want to explain everything at once, but it's not making any sense and my insides are tightening up.

"Bring them in, quickly," says Nahul's ma, putting her arms around us. "She looks like she's going to collapse."

I feel myself swaying, and then everything goes black.

CHAPTER

22

Low voices come to me in waves, and when I open my eyes I see Jeevan next to me. Both of us are propped up on cushions and sheepskins beside a roaring open fire.

"Don't be afraid," says Nahul's ma, leaning over me. "It's Asha, isn't it?"

I'm overcome with exhaustion, unable to keep my eyes from sliding shut, so I dig my nails into my palms to force myself to stay awake.

"Teenu," she says to a little girl. "Come and sit beside me."

The whole family gathers in front of the fire, staring at us inquisitively.

"Now, where did you find these children, Nahul?" asks his papa. "So far from anywhere."

"In the forest," he says. "There was a tiger."

His ma clamps her hands to her mouth.

"No one was harmed, Ma . . . In fact, we think the tiger saved Jeevan from being attacked by wolves . . . Tell them what happened, Asha."

"Let them eat something . . . all this talking," says Nahul's grandmother. She ladles two bowls of cinnamon-scented stew from the pot above the fire, hands me one, and straightaway begins spooning tiny amounts into Jeevan's mouth, which he swallows slowly. I warm my frozen hands around the bowl.

Everyone is watching me expectantly. I try to concentrate but my eyes are drooping.

"Wh-when we arrived at the shelter I knew something was wrong," I begin, reliving the intense fear I sensed the moment we approached the clearing.

Between us, Nahul and I begin telling them the

story—how the horse was skittish, how the tiger was standing in front of the shelter, bloodstains in the snow, how I picked up a log from the fire and Nahul fired a shot—and how we found a dead wolf nearby.

Everyone is absolutely silent, their eyes wide.

"Perhaps it was the spirit of an ancestor," says Nahul's grandmother, pausing in her task of feeding Jeevan.

"The tiger had the same eyes as Asha," Nahul adds eagerly. His grandmother nods. I wonder if it's true, if another of my ancestors was watching over me. I touch my pendant, feeling the rhythms of generations past.

"You have the gift, my child," she says to me. With her free hand she flips my palms over and traces my lines with a rough finger. I shiver, reminded of our visit to the witch at the very start of our journey. "Yes, you are an adventurer . . . lots of journeys here."

Jeevan hasn't spoken the whole time, and suddenly I realize that he's burning up again, falling asleep.

Nahul's grandmother has noticed too, and she sets the bowl down.

"I'll boil some hot ginger and tulsi tea," she says gravely.

Jeevan's entire weight pushes against me and his cheeks glow hot, and silently I beg him not to die.

CHAPTER

23

It's been four nights. Divali is only a little more than four weeks away and we must leave for the temple today if we're going to have a chance of reaching Papa on time. Jeevan's fever has gone, but is he really strong enough to carry on?

It's morning, and while he's still sleeping, I untie my bundle of things, pulling out my journey clothes: the jeans and green hoodie. I yank them on before trying to wake him.

"We have to go," I say, shaking Jeevan gently. I try to be as patient as I can but hardly sound it.

He doesn't stir, so I shake him some more. "Jeevan . . . Jeevan."

He wakes up. Traces of the dark fever circles are still visible below his eyes, and I feel bad for not letting him sleep longer.

"Jeevan," I say with a pretend lightness. "What if you stayed here . . . and let me go on by myself?"

"What?" He sits up suddenly. "You can't do that—"

"Look," I say gently, kneeling on the rug. "I'm worried about you . . . You're not that strong and it's still a long way to Zandapur." I stand up, turning away from him, because I can't bear to look him in the eye. "Maybe you could stay with the family for a bit longer." I pause. "A-and then get the train back to Sonahaar."

"No way, Asha—I'm coming with you," he says fiercely. "All for one and one for all—remember? I heard how you built that shelter in the forest . . . and the way you fought off the tiger." He sounds annoyed. "And I know you're getting so good at doing things by yourself now . . . but we have to stay together till the end." He gives me a hard stare, then tosses his head away. "Unless . . . you don't need me anymore."

"No! You know that's not true. I can't manage without you. I'm just really worried that you could get ill again."

Jeevan turns away from me. "Only if you're sure . . . I don't want to be a *burden*," he mumbles stubbornly.

I force him to face me. "Yes, of course I'm sure . . . Please, Jeevan, I need you . . . Let's collect our things and get ready." I feel so guilty for even suggesting he stay behind. I put my hand on his shoulder. "You must tell me if you need to rest . . . I promise I'll listen."

"And we have to stay friends this time, be kind to each other," says Jeevan, spreading the scarf out on the floor. "*However* hard things get."

"Yes . . . You're right," I say, giving him a hug. "Here, you load up while I pass you the things." I pick up the mango stone, still safe in its banana leaf pot. "It hasn't grown any shoots yet." I hold it up to the light just in case I've missed something. "Tuck it in safely."

"All you can do is keep watering it—you never know; it might grow."

The horse is already whinnying outside, which

means everyone is awake, preparing for the day ahead. I kiss Papa's letter and stow it safely in my pocket.

"There, it's all ready," Jeevan says, slotting the penknife into the pile of things.

We go outside, where Nahul's papa is grooming the horse. Nahul fiddles with the stirrup and looks in my direction, but I avoid his gaze and kick at the frosty ground, trying to shake away his ebony eyes.

He doesn't say anything, just concentrates on stroking the horse's flank.

"So . . . you're ready?" asks Nahul's papa.

"Yes," I say. "Are you OK, Jeevan?"

"You don't have to worry about me," he says, shooting me an irritated look. "I'm feeling fine."

Nahul takes a carved wooden elephant from his pocket and thrusts it into my hand. "I made it myself." He blushes.

I give a shy smile as I take it. "Thank you." I hold it in my palm, admiring the delicate trunk that points to the sky. "I'll treasure it always."

Jeevan looks sulky, turns as if to say something to me, but stays tight-lipped.

"And this is for Jeevan . . . to keep him warm." Nahul holds out a goatskin jacket.

"Er . . . thank you." He slips it on. "Thank you all."

"Wait," calls Teenu, running up to us, carrying two flower garlands. "These are for your journey."

Nahul lifts her up so she can reach us.

"Grandmother helped me . . . I hope you find your papa." She raises the white bakul flowers and puts them around our necks.

The garland's sweet incense-like smell surrounds me. "Thank you for everything. You've been so kind and generous."

They all give a final wave as we turn to leave.

"We won't forget you," says Jeevan, ignoring Nahul and looking across to the rest of the family.

"Keep walking toward the peaks," says Nahul's papa. "And once you start the climb you'll see prayer flags all along the path to the temple—they'll guide your journey. Stay alert. Lack of food is bringing the snow leopards lower down."

Jeevan and I exchange a fearful look. "We will," we say, finally turning away from the house, keeping the impressive mountain range straight in front of us, its layers of snow making it shine like a flashing diamond in the sun.

My breath blows ahead of me like woodsmoke and I pull my sleeves over my hands to keep them warm. The early-morning fog rises in swirls from the valley below as we concentrate on walking as quickly as we can.

We eventually reach a steep, rugged slope edged with pines, where a sign for Kasare points upward. We begin the climb to the temple and I stretch up and sling Jeevan's arm around my shoulder.

He pulls away. "Thank you for looking after me . . . but I'm not a baby, you know. I'm much stronger now."

"Come on, grumpy guts," I tease. "You were right about staying together and I'm glad it's just the two of us again."

We clamber farther and farther toward the temple, the clear blue sky stretching ahead of us like a never-ending piece of silk.

"I think we'll be there before dark if we carry on walking this quickly," I say, assessing the height of the sun. "But if you need a rest, you must tell me . . . You will, won't you?"

"Promise," he says.

Just as Nahul's papa said, there are colorful prayer flags tied to the lower branches of the trees.

Jeevan is full of life, just like before, his shoulders back as if he could walk forever.

"Look at you, steaming ahead."

"See, I told you."

We continue walking steadily upward, until the outline of a figure bent over a stick appears ahead of us. As we get closer I see it's an old woman wearing an orange sari.

"Namaste," I say, raising my hands to her. With the flower garland that Teenu gave me this morning and my short hair, I feel like I fit perfectly on the route to the temple.

She raises her hands back to us and smiles as we pass.

The air gets even colder the higher we climb, the golden sun dropping to the west, and I pull my hoodie tight around myself as we keep clambering on.

My legs are suddenly heavy and each step is more difficult to take, the gravel scraping under my feet as I force myself up the curve of the mountain path. I stop to catch my breath but when we turn the next corner, there in the bluish haze of early evening is my spirit bird, hovering in the biting breeze.

"Jeevan, look!" I cry in surprise. "Remember I told you there was a bird that came into the forest . . . when you were ill?" I glance across at his expression to guess what he thinks. "It perched on the shelter while I was away . . . My nanijee's spirit is looking after us."

"It would be good if she was," he says, picking up his pace. "But let's get to the temple. That's what we need to focus on."

I suppose I can't expect him to feel the same magic as me, but I'm disappointed all the same. He's still so matter-of-fact about it, despite everything that's happened.

The lamagaia glides over us and lands on a rock balanced on the ridge ahead.

A shot of energy comes from nowhere and suddenly I feel I have wings. I hardly notice my ragged breathing as I reach the ridge ahead of Jeevan . . . and there it is at last! The temple!

I fall to my knees and touch my forehead to the stony ground in prayer.

"This is where Shiva threw his hair into the Ganges," I say, totally in awe, rising to my feet again. "Can you believe we're here?"

It's more magnificent than anything I've ever seen before. Carved from an iridescent rose-colored rock, the temple has four spiraling turrets, which almost disappear into the sky, and in the center a wide dome covered in pale orange-colored tiles sparkles like a rising sun.

Jeevan grabs me by the arms and begins swinging me around. "Asha! We're here, we're here, we're here!" he sings.

"We've done it," we whisper together, looking down on the temple, our voices rising into the twilight.

A pathway runs from the top of the ridge down to the imposing arched doorway of the temple, which has colored glass windows on either side. The tiny ochre lights from the deevay glow yellow, pink, and blue, and have been placed everywhere to welcome the pilgrims.

My chest is filled with bubbles of excitement, which fizz and flutter as it sinks in that I'm really here.

My nanijee is still on the ridge next to us and I hold out my hands toward her, bringing them together in thanks. She stays for a moment longer before soaring above the temple, the air whooshing behind her, her wings outstretched in splendor, and then she disappears into the snow-white clouds.

"See?" I say. "It *is* her!"

"Mmm... maybe... or maybe it's a temple bird used to getting all the tidbits from the pilgrims."

"Oh, Jeevan!"

Prayer flags in all the colors of the rainbow are strung across the front of the temple, and towering behind it, covered in violet-white snow, is the colossal mountain— the mountain where the Holy Ganges is born.

I slip my hand into Jeevan's, and together we follow the path down to the temple. We cross the threshold through to a vast hall with smooth marble floors. It's filled with people sitting cross-legged, their heads bowed and their eyes closed in prayer.

I brush the dust off my clothes and straighten my

top, feeling the short hairs on the back of my head prickle with nerves.

The hall is glowing with candles and more deevay, the air scented with sandalwood mixed with woody patchouli and rose.

"Can you believe even those old women climbed all the way here?" says Jeevan loudly.

"Don't stare!" I hiss, stooping down, feeling a pang of embarrassment as I pull off my dirty, torn sneakers and line them up next to the chappala—the gold-embroidered shoes and the worn leather slippers that belong to all the other pilgrims.

Jeevan unties his laces hurriedly. "Shall we do the rituals as soon as we can? Then we can leave first thing in the morning and head straight to the city."

"Slow down! You're always in such a rush."

"Sorry, Asha." He tugs my sleeve. "I know this is important."

"No . . . You're right. We can't waste a minute. Who knows what's happened to Papa. We'll do the rituals tonight and be ready for Zandapur tomorrow." My heart gives a patter.

CHAPTER
24

"he source of the Ganges must be over there,"
whispers Jeevan, looking toward a line of
people that snakes its way along one side of
the hall.

We get behind a man wearing nothing but a dhoti,
the length of bright orange fabric wrapped around his
waist and twisted through his legs to make a typical
yogi's outfit.

"He must be freezing . . . Look at his hair!" I say.

It falls all the way down to the floor in long, matted
locks.

"I bet he's spent all his life visiting temples," says

Jeevan, beaming from ear to ear. "I wouldn't enjoy brushing that, though!"

I nudge Jeevan. "Shhh . . ."

There's a priest at the head of the line wearing orange flowing robes that skim the ground. He dips his fingers into a brass bowl and flicks holy water over the milling crowds. "Blessings . . . blessings," he calls. "Blessings to all the pilgrims who've made this journey." He hurls rose and marigold petals into the air. "The Holy Ganges honors her visitors."

The sound of the roaring water becomes louder as we move closer to the front of the line.

"I'm going to say prayers for my brother as well as my ma and papa," says Jeevan.

"I think he'd really like that."

We link arms and together we approach the exact spot where the Ganges is born.

"Welcome," says the priest, giving us a smile that makes his eyes almost disappear. "Where are your parents?"

"We've traveled here together," says Jeevan. "And we're on our way to Zandapur, to find Asha's papa."

"Yes . . . I'm Asha, and this is Jeevan."

"And we're from Moormanali," he says.

"So, Jeevan and Asha." The priest picks up a gleaming silver bowl, dips his finger into it, and paints thick red dye between my eyebrows and then Jeevan's. "Here's your red pilgrim's mark. Now everyone will know what you've done and how far you've been."

"Thank you." I bow my head, breathing deeply, and move farther forward toward the source.

At last we're right at the very spot where the River Ganges springs from a rose-colored rock and cascades into a huge marble-edged pool. There are pilgrims bathing right below the opening, which is about five times as wide as my outstretched arms.

The water splashes everywhere, sending fine, lacy mist traveling up into the air. "Look how fierce it is," I say, mesmerized.

"Wow . . . How do you think they built this temple all the way up here?" asks Jeevan. "All I'd need is a boat and the water could take me straight into the whole of India."

"Don't be silly!" I giggle. "It'd take forever to get

around the whole of India . . . shall we do our offer-ings now?"

I place the flower garland that Nahul's little sister, Teenu, gave me on the floor and take a space next to Jeevan beside the pool.

I slip my hand into the bundle and search for the braid I cut off in Sonahaar and carried all the way especially for this moment. I hold it coiled in my palm, ready to offer it up.

I close my eyes and meditate on my offering for the Holy River Ganges, the Daughter of the Mountain.

I clasp the pendant to my chest and try to connect with the spirit of my nanijee and all the daughters in my family who've ever worn the necklace before me. I feel the ancient rhythms spanning across time, reach-ing out to me, as if I could almost touch them with my fingertips.

Please, Daughter of the Mountain, I bring this offering to you as I have seen in my visions.

I have come to honor you,

Just as you came to earth to help us in the past.

Will you come to my aid now?

Lead me to Papa,

Please let my family be reunited.

Give blessings to all those who have helped me,

Above all for my friend Jeevan . . . I especially thank you for saving his life. Without his help I could never have made this journey,

And for my dear nanijee and all the daughters of my family.

I place my feet at the edge of the pool, my toes curled around the smooth marble rim, and jump in, releasing my braid into the icy water. The holy water covers me completely, swallowing me up in its swirls of cascading froth, my lungs gripped by iron fingers, the freezing shock sucking away my breath.

The water parts as I burst back to the surface just in time to see my dark braid of hair disappear through the channel and make its way outside, where the Holy River Ganges—filled with snowmelt and monsoon storms—will carry it down the mountainside.

Cold drops of water bead and drip over my head and onto my face. I'm standing shoulder-deep in the pool, my teeth chattering. "Jeevan . . . Can you pass me the deeva? Be careful not to let it go out."

He takes the clay deeva in the palm of his hand and slowly holds it toward me.

I lean across to the garland, pluck a white flower, place it in the deeva, and float it in the pool, pressing my palms together to finish the ritual.

"It's your turn now." I lift myself out and sit on the edge, my breath rising and falling in time to my dancing heart.

Jeevan gives a worried smile. "Do you think my ma will be proud of me?"

"Of course she will, Jeevan—she'll be amazed by what you've done . . . I promise."

"Here goes, then . . . bath time!" Jeevan jumps into the pool, vanishing beneath the bubbling water for a few moments, then stands in the water, closes his eyes, and says his prayers.

As my thoughts drift to Papa in Zandapur, then to Ma back home, I feel warm, familiar hands on my shoulders . . .

Asha, Asha, Asha, my love,
The thunder brought you,
For me to love.

Do you remember how you asked me to sing this over and over again so you wouldn't have to go back to the dreams of past lives that woke you screaming in the middle of the night?

I held you close and you traced the bumpy veins in my old, wrinkled hands, telling me they were the rivers flowing down to the sea.

I feel a blanket wrapped around me and everything is perfect, like the warmth of sunshine when your eyelids are closed. My pendant rocks . . .

Nanijee?

I look around, scanning the hall for the soft folds of her embroidered sari where I used to hide, her song still echoing in my head, but there's no one there.

Jeevan gets out of the water and sits beside me. "It's so cold," he says, shivering, tying his hair back into the topknot. Little strands have come loose and stick to his face. "What's the matter?" he asks.

"S-something strange just happened. I think my nanijee was here." I stare back into the pool.

"Really?"

I blink and take a deep breath. "Maybe everything

will turn out right after all." I pull an edge of the blanket and tuck it around his shoulder. "She put this on me. I was shivering."

"It was probably the priest."

"Why do you never believe me?"

"It's not that I don't believe you." He tightens the blanket. "We're just different . . . It would be boring if we were all the same, wouldn't it?" He nudges me. "I'm Mr. Science, remember?"

"Yeah, exactly."

I take out the mango stone I planted at the beginning of our journey and place it beside me as I listen to the pilgrims chanting. The golden glow of all the deevay shimmering in the water makes everything look magical.

I bend toward the banana leaf pot, looking for any sign of a shoot, but the soil is still bare. "Maybe the holy water will make you grow." I scoop a palmful of the cold Ganges water and sprinkle it over the soil, patting it with my fingers. "There . . . Grow, little mango, grow for Papa." I blink my eyes closed and carry on listening to the sounds of the temple, thinking about

Nanijee and all my ancestors, feeling the rhythms pulling me away into their spirit world.

Jeevan touches my shoulder and I come back with a start.

"Shall we get changed? I'm frozen."

I pick up the mango pot, nestling it between my hands, and sense a warmth passing through the damp banana leaf. I give it a final sprinkle of water, wrinkling my nose in pleasure as the smell of the damp earth reminds me of early morning, walking barefoot with Papa on the grazing pastures.

Jeevan pulls me to my feet. "Hurry up . . . You look like you've been sleeping. I'm starving."

I'm still in a daze as we walk toward a doorway and are greeted by smells of spiced dhal and freshly baked naan. "This way," calls a woman. "Towels are on the side and then you can sit for food over there."

Once we're dry we squeeze between the others and sit cross-legged, eating our food from shiny thalia.

My heart feels like it is full of singing birds that will burst into the room at any moment, filling the temple with happiness.

I look up toward a small set of windows with carvings of Lord Shiva's story all around them at the very top of the large hall. Through one of them I can see the tiniest slice of moon hanging in the darkness. It shines onto the mango pot, bathing it in its silvered light.

"Jeevan, look! When we started our journey the moon was full and now it's nearly starting out again . . . like us."

"That means we've been away from Moormanali for almost two whole weeks," he replies, scooping rice into his mouth. "It feels like months, though." He shifts his gaze down to my side. "So your mango stone's sprouted, then."

"What?" I pick up the stone, which a moment ago had nothing growing from it, and lift it to the light. "That's amazing! It must have been the holy water and all my praying that made it happen." It has a strong green shoot about the size of my finger and two tender fresh leaves either side.

"Plants store up their energy and then, when the conditions are right, they spring into life," Jeevan says, stuffing more food into his mouth.

"No, Jeevan! It was the praying and the water and my nanijee that have made it grow so quickly." I can feel a broad grin spreading across my face. "It's sprouted and that's all that matters."

I put the seedling back into the moonlight, its shadow stretching across the marble floor.

"We'll leave for Zandapur tomorrow. And just think, it's four whole weeks till Divali and probably only a few days before we find Papa and bring him home."

"That will be amazing, won't it?" says Jeevan. "Just imagine the look on your ma's face when you appear back in Moormanali with your papa by your side!"

CHAPTER
25

Early the next morning, we collect our things and kneel to say one last prayer before setting off for Zandapur. I try to gather my thoughts into neat little piles but my mind keeps skipping from one thing to another, then back to Moormanali. Has Ma written back to Uncle Neel yet? My stomach clenches . . . I must hurry and find Papa.

We join a group of pilgrims and walk away from the temple, flicking glances toward the bushy pine trees.

"We can't believe you came all this way by your-selves," says a woman wrapped in a pink woolen shawl.

"It takes some people their whole lives to make a trip to this temple, and you've done it already."

"The spirit of my nanijee makes me strong," I say.

"But *you* had to decide to come," says Jeevan.

"Yes . . . Ma said I have to work out what I believe for myself, and that's exactly what I did . . . And you came with me. So maybe it's a mixture of things."

The woman with the shawl laughs. "Who knows whether our ancestors are really with us. But they do say that some people can feel their presence."

We carry on walking along the path, listening to the birds of prey sending out their echoing calls from way up in the sky. I keep looking around, expecting to see my spirit bird again and thinking about Nanijee, feeling stronger and more determined to find Papa and bring him home before Meena and her thugs return.

"Asha?" says Jeevan. "Are you scared about what we might find in the city?"

I tug at the ties to my hood. "Part of me is worried about what we'll find once we get there . . . I mean, why hasn't he written?" And what if the truth is even harder than not knowing?

Jeevan moves closer. "We won't know anything until we find him . . . and we can't change what's happened. But when he sees what you've done and how far you've come, he'll think you're the most courageous daughter he could ever wish for . . . like Sita with her bow and arrow, or Durga fighting off the demons!"

"Really?"

"Really. I mean, look at all the hard stuff we've done."

"Maybe you're right." I look toward the dark outline of the pines against the morning sun. "It's not over yet, though. We still have to get down the mountain safely," I say, the memory of what happened in the forest gripping my throat.

It's early afternoon by the time we get to the road and it feels strange to be surrounded by buses and cars again after the peacefulness of the temple.

"Let's share a drink." I walk over to one of the stalls. "We haven't spent much money and Zandapur's not far now, so I think we'll have enough."

"Asha . . . postcards. Let's send another one home."

I count my coins. "OK . . . What about this one of the temple?" I pick it up and pay.

We write the postcard quickly and slip it into the postbox. As we turn away with our drinks I catch sight of something that turns my mouth dry and sets my heart pounding.

"Jeevan, look at that poster!"

MISSING

TWELVE-YEAR-OLD
JEEVAN SINGH GILL

AND

ELEVEN-YEAR-OLD
ASHA KUMAR

IF YOU HAVE ANY INFORMATION
CONTACT THE POLICE.

He splutters his drink on the ground. "Keep your head down."

I study the small poster. "These photos don't look anything like us."

"Well, that boy recognized you." He pulls the poster off the tree and stuffs it into his pocket. "Now that we're getting closer to Zandapur there will be more police everywhere."

One of the pilgrims calls us over. "That blue bus will take you right into Zandapur," she says, pointing to one that's already rammed with people. "Look after each other and be careful in the city—it's full of all sorts of people, not all of them good."

"We will," I say.

The pilgrim presses a few coins into my palm. "Bless you on your journey, little ones."

"Thank you," says Jeevan, the corners of his mouth curling into a smile.

My insides are starting to twist and turn as I climb onto the crowded bus, pulling my hood up to hide my face.

"Go there," says Jeevan, pointing to a space right at the back.

The bus begins to hum and shake as the driver

turns the engine. A cold breeze blows in through the open door and we pull out of the small tangle of stalls and shops before turning at a big sign that says ZANDAPUR.

It doesn't take long before we're on a road that twists dangerously down steep rocky gorges. There are views for miles of wooded valleys full of dark pines and crashing waterfalls.

"Once we get to Zandapur, we need to be very careful who we trust. Just imagine if I could control my dream visions—I'd be able to see the faces of all the evil people in the city and keep us safe."

"Now that *would* be handy." Jeevan snuggles deeper into his seat. "Asha, how do you know whether to believe something you dream about?"

"It's strange." I look out the window. "Some dreams are really clear, like the one about the journey to find Papa. I try to work them out."

"So they're a bit like a puzzle."

"Yes, I suppose you could say that." I think about Nanijee and what I felt at the temple. "And then there are some things that you just can't explain . . . like the bell moving all by itself in the cowshed before Meena and those men came."

"If you really tried," says Jeevan, "maybe you could actually make stuff happen . . . like maybe you could force that man to give me his paratha."

"Don't be ridiculous, Jeevan. I wish I *could* control things," I say, yawning. "But for now I think I'm too tired."

The next time I open my eyes, there are cars, cows, and people everywhere. Outside, the light is fading, turning into evening. "Where are we?"

"We're in Zandapur," says Jeevan. "Come on, sleepyhead," he laughs. "You look like you're still dreaming."

"Yes," I say slowly, getting out of the seat. "Something was just about to happen . . . but everything disappeared." I follow him down the aisle, trying to remember. "There were children . . . lots and lots of—"

"Don't worry about the dream now," Jeevan interrupts me, and we step into the busy bus station full of people laughing, talking, shouting. There are so many signs and everyone's moving so quickly.

Jeevan grabs hold of my arm and pulls me back onto

the sidewalk just before a bus spewing smoke out of the back rattles by. "This isn't the village," he says. "We've got to have our wits about us—that bus nearly squashed you."

I take a deep breath and concentrate.

"Which way is the right way"—Jeevan looks confused—"when we don't know where we're going?"

"I *do* know where we're going," I say. "Connaught Place. And I want to get there as soon as I can." We're here at last, so close to Papa, and I let my heart give a little leap as I imagine seeing him again, but a knot of fear follows close behind—I'll soon find out why he stopped writing.

A youngish man is looking at the timetable, chewing gum. He spits on the floor and spins around to face us. "Looking for somewhere to stay? My uncle's got a hotel near here. Cheap. Good for boys like you."

I lower my voice. "We're meeting my papa here. He's coming any minute."

The man looks us up and down and kicks a plastic cup. "Are you sure?" he asks, dialing a number before putting a small phone to his ear. "Very cheap."

"We're sure." I pull Jeevan away. "We'll ask someone else in a minute," I whisper. "He was really creepy."

We hurry through a dark archway that opens into a tunnel leading away from the station.

"I want to find Connaught Place before nightfall." The tunnel is gloomy and smells worse than old fish. "The sooner we find Papa, the sooner we can get back to Moormanali. There won't be a moon tomorrow, you know. That means it's four weeks until Divali."

"It won't take us that long to find your papa and get home in time," says Jeevan. "Maybe your ma won't even have replied to your uncle Neel yet."

I feel excited. "Do you think we'll all be back together for my birthday?"

"Yes," says Jeevan. "Definitely."

CHAPTER
26

I buzz with fear as we walk through the dark tunnel toward the center of Zandapur, empty wrappers and plastic bags whirling toward us on the wind. I pause to wipe grit from my eyes.

A little girl sits in the shadow of the arches, holding out a dirt-crusted hand. "Paisa, paisa," she calls to us in a pleading voice. Her eyes are huge and dark, and tangled hair hangs in clumps around her shoulders.

"That girl's only about Rohan and Roopa's age, maybe even younger. Where's her family?" I feel so angry. "It's so wrong for her to be doing this."

"I know," says Jeevan. "But this is how some families survive in the city."

People dressed in smart suits and fancy saris walk past without even glancing at her. "Surely they could spare at least one coin!" I take one from my purse and place it in her hand.

"Thank you," she says, giving us a small smile.

As we turn into an even busier street, a giant poster surrounded by bright lights beams down at us. A banner across the top says:

RECYCLE-REUSE-REPURPOSE
CITY DUMP
WE TURN YOUR TRASH INTO GOLD

But underneath it I spot something else. "A map," I say, pulling Jeevan toward it. "Let's find Connaught Place."

The map is a confusion of streets that crisscross each other. "Here's the bus station," says Jeevan. "But I can't see Connaught Place."

"It has to be here somewhere," I say, studying it in frustration.

"Unless it's not right in the center," says Jeevan.

A group of men come walking toward us, drinking from dark bottles, arguing and yelling at each other.

"They look like real losers," I say, pulling Jeevan closer and linking our arms.

"Don't worry . . . We'll ask someone . . . Let's cross over," he says, pulling me closer.

We dodge mustard-yellow taxis and bullock carts to reach the opposite sidewalk.

A sudden clap of thunder cracks above the noise of the traffic, and it starts pouring down.

"Quick, let's go in there." We head toward a café with a bright sign in the window showing a boy eating something delicious. "We'll be out of the rain and can sit down and decide how to find Papa." Jeevan still looks thin from his fever—I have to make sure he eats, so he doesn't get sick again.

"Yeah . . . I could do with some food," he says, leaning against the doors to open them.

Inside, the café is full of young people sitting at

small tables, laughing and munching on round bread with something stuffed inside.

"It's called 'fast food,'" says Jeevan, reading an electric sign behind the counter.

A sweet, oily smell floats through the air. "Maybe you eat here after you've been fasting?"

"Yeah, could be."

"It says two for the price of one." I notice a handwritten poster next to the counter. I peer inside my purse, bubbling with excitement. "That means we can eat something and still have a bit of money left for a taxi. Sit over there by the window. I'll line up for the food."

Jeevan pushes our bundle onto a bench and lets out a sigh as he slides in next to it.

The restaurant feels like a safe place, full of people having fun, and I start to relax a little. Jeevan gives me a wave as I get closer to the counter and I smile back at him.

When it's my turn to order I'm not sure what to ask for, so I show the girl the things I want in the picture behind her. She hands me a tray with food all wrapped up in paper, like little presents.

"Have a nice day," she says, taking my money.

I plonk the tray down in front of Jeevan and sit beside him.

"Wow." He stares at everything as if he wants to gobble it all down in one go.

I dunk my finger into the soft, fluffy drink and lick the delicious creamy liquid, then I take a bite of the bouncy bread and crunchy vegetable burger inside it. "Mmm . . . this tastes so good." I chew slowly, savoring the new flavors.

"Oh yeah . . . It's amazing." Jeevan crams the bread into his mouth and stuffs the straw in at the same time, slurping the drink noisily.

Once we've finished I empty my purse onto the tray. "Now, let's see how much money we've got left."

"What about getting one of those yellow taxis?" asks Jeevan. "That way we'll get straight to where your papa is."

"I'm not sure how much it'll cost, but I hope we have enough." I count the coins and the rupee notes. "Oh, Jeevan, I can't believe we're going to find him at last."

"I know . . . After everything we've been through."

He nudges me with his elbow. "It's actually going to happen."

"But let's wait until the rain stops." Outside the window a row of people have gathered and are slumped against the café, pulling dirty blankets over themselves to shelter from the rain that's still lashing hard against the glass. I shudder and split the rest of my meal with Jeevan and we eat as slowly as possible, staying a little longer.

One of the waiters starts to clear our table. "You can't stay here all night," he says roughly, picking the tray up.

"We know that, sir," I say, trying to be as polite as I can. "But it's just that it's raining so hard."

"Come on, get out of here!"

"OK," says Jeevan, grabbing our things. "There's no need to be rude, we're going . . . come on, Asha."

I stare at the rain flowing like a river outside and slowly open the door.

A crowded taxi zooms past, soaking us with muddy water. "Yech . . . How are we going to get one of these taxis to stop?" I ask. "They're hardly going to pay any attention to two kids like us."

"I'm not sure," Jeevan says, looking around.

"Excuse me, darlings." A young woman appears from nowhere and sidles up to us. "My name's Nina. I'm new in the city and I'm looking for a good place to stay. Do you know anywhere?"

"I—I'm Jeevan." His voice has gone all stuttery.

The woman smells of perfume and carries a fancy leather handbag. I wonder if she might be an actress. Krishen, who gave us a lift in his truck, said Zandapur was full of them.

"We're new ourselves," I say. "So I'm afraid we can't help you."

"We're trying to get a taxi to stop," says Jeevan.

"Would you like to share one?" She gives a shiny smile. "That way I can find a hotel and it will be cheaper for you . . . Two boys like you shouldn't be hanging around in the dark by yourselves, you know."

Jeevan turns his back to her and moves closer to where I'm standing. "What do you think?" he whispers.

My pendant hangs heavy and strange against my

chest. "I know she seems nice and everything...but let's find our own taxi."

"What are you two whispering about?" She puts her arms around our shoulders and pulls us gently toward her. "How old are you? Let me guess... Thirteen? I've got a little brother just like you." She hooks her finger under Jeevan's chin. "Look, you won't get any of these taxis to stop for you...How about we jump in this one?" She waves her arm into the road. "I bet you've never been in one of these yellow ambassadors."

I swallow, my heart thudding, feeling like I need to run, but she's got her arm tight around us again and the taxi has already slowed to a halt, pushing open the door so we can't get past.

"Come on, it'll be fine...I promise." She's speaking quickly now and shoves us into the waiting taxi, squeezes in beside us, and slams the door shut.

We're barely in the car before it swerves onto the road, sending us flying across the slippery seats. Fear grips me.

The woman gives a high laugh. "First to one of the

central hotels and then wherever these boys are going."
She opens her bag. "I'll pay."

"Jeevan," I say under my breath. "I want to get out."
He's not listening to me, though—he's watching as the
lady pulls out a small box with gold writing all over it.
"The best barfi in the whole of the city." She opens it,
offering us a chunk.

Jeevan puts his hand in straightaway and stuffs one
into his mouth. "Mmm . . ." he says, chewing. "Delicious."

"And a special one for you," she says, pulling out a
triangle of barfi with shiny silver leaf painted onto it.
She crams it into my mouth.

"Go on, Asha . . . It's so yummy."

"No!" I protest, grabbing her arm. "Stop it. I don't
want it!" I swipe the barfi onto the floor, spitting out
the bits she stuffed into my mouth.

"There's no need to get angry . . . I'm only being
kind." She takes out a red lipstick and begins stroking
it on. "Look, your friend is tired."

"Yeah." Jeevan begins to yawn, blinking his eyes as if
he's having trouble keeping them open. "Tha . . . w . . .
was r . . . ude . . ."

"He's so sleepy," the woman says, flipping open her phone, jabbing at the buttons.

I press my face against the cold window and bang on the glass but the taxi driver goes faster than ever.

Jeevan slumps against the car door.

"What's happened to you?" I shake him, but his arm is floppy and nothing I do makes him wake up.

The taxi skids to a halt in front of a rundown building that looks nothing like a hotel. A man standing in the shadows of the doorway makes my heart pound so fiercely I think it might crack . . .

I grip the edge of the seat, frozen.

He counts out some notes and hands them to the woman. And that's when I know for sure that we've been tricked.

The car door is wide open—it's my only chance—but Jeevan is fast asleep. I'll come back for him. I can't let us both be taken by these people, whoever they are. I leap out of the taxi and run into the dead of night.

I've no idea where I'm going. Filthy puddles splash up my legs and my breath stings my lungs as I race away with only one thought in my head: I have to escape.

Heavy footsteps slam behind me, and my heart flies into my mouth. "Stop!" My hood is yanked backward, burning my neck. "Come here!"

I'm hoisted up and flipped upside down across the man's thick shoulders, sending my head crashing against his back.

"Let me go!" I yell, banging my fists.

He throws me onto the wet ground, wraps a stinking cloth around my eyes, and pulls it tight.

"No more funny business," he says, shoving me forward.

"Where's Jeevan?" I shout, clawing at his arms. "What have you done with him?"

"Shut it!" yells the man, slapping me across the face.

The sting of his heavy palm makes me cry out.

His knuckles dig deep into my back as I'm propelled forward and shuffled along in front of him, tears collecting behind the blindfold . . . What is this? Where am I?

I hear the sharp sound of a key twisting in a lock,

then feel a foot in the base of my spine, pushing me forward, and I land on the ground with a smack, my mouth filling with the iron tang of blood.

The door slams and locks.

There are only four weeks left until Divali, and I know that I've failed. I'll never find Papa and get home in time. All I've done is make things worse.

CHAPTER

27

I spend all night with my chin pressed into my knees, in a corner of the room. I'm terrified of what's going to happen next and what they're going to do with me. My head pounds with the sound of their jagged voices that slink back to haunt me.

Eventually a dull gleam of weak light struggles in through the small glassless window near the ceiling, casting shadows around the filthy room. It's little more than a cupboard, full of dark cobwebbed corners, and smells as if it's been used as a toilet, turning last night's food into bile in my mouth.

On the floor, the mango seedling and my feather lie

discarded on the grimy ground where they were tossed out of my bundle last night. A man rifled through my things, taking Jeevan's penknife and the last of my money. One of the seedling's newly sprouted leaves has been knocked off and the other one is crushed and torn.

I scoop up the soil from the ground with my fingers and refold the leaf around the stone. An angry tear escapes onto the seedling as I tuck it safely into the front pocket of my jeans before tying Papa's scarf around my neck.

I clutch my pendant, willing it to respond, and pray for its rhythm to give me strength. I try to feel for the memories—a sign that I haven't been entirely abandoned—but there's nothing. Jeevan was right all along: It's just my imagination.

I beat back the tears because now, more than ever, I have to be strong, just like I was before, when Ma told me to believe in myself. I gather my courage and make a promise, even though I don't know how I'll do it: *I'm going to find Jeevan and get us both out of here.*

. . .

They come for me soon after, two men who push me out into a huge open yard with a great gray mound at its center. Out here it smells worse than ever, like all the world's most rotten things gathered together in one place. A stream of vomit escapes from my mouth and I swallow the bitter remains, wiping saliva with the back of my hand.

"Keep moving." One man prods me in the back with a whip and I stumble forward.

Climbing all over the gigantic mound are small groups of children, maybe as many as two whole classes at school. Their heads are bent low as they pick through paper and plastic, collecting it into huge sacks that are strapped to their backs.

"You're to sort the trash; pick out metals, electrical wires, and glass bottles. And especially anything that looks valuable. Any nonsense"—the man scowls—"and you'll feel how hard this whip is. Got it?"

I block my nose at the stench.

"Get used to it." He sniggers, pushing the whip into my shoulder. "You'll be here for a long time."

None of the other children speak or look at me as I

walk toward them, and the reason, I see straightaway, is that there are more men with hard faces who march around the junkyard, brandishing long whips, hurling abuse at everyone.

A towering brick wall with razor wire along the top stretches all the way around us. *Don't cry*, I tell myself, desperately twisting the corners of the sack I've been given. *Crying won't get us out of here.* But the wall is so high, there's no way I could climb it.

The ground below my feet is unstable and each step I take makes me sink farther into the mass of slush. I begin to collect the shards of metal that spike into my thin sneakers and drop them into the sack, slipping one into my pocket in case I need it later.

I scan the junkyard, searching for Jeevan everywhere, but I can't see him.

One of the men throws an old shoe, which hits a boy on the leg. The boy clasps his leg in pain and cries out, but everyone carries on working; not a single person looks at him or bothers to see if he's all right.

When I finally spot Jeevan on the far side of the mound, the tight knots in my stomach uncurl and

I want to rush over immediately, let him know I'm still alive, but instead I tread cautiously toward him, afraid that they'll lock me away again.

I pick at pieces of trash with my stick, keeping my eyes fixed on Jeevan, pretending to search for the things I've been told to as I steadily move closer to him . . .

It's only when I'm nearly there that I dare to let out a whisper. "Jeevan!" I keep my head down. "Over here."

He looks up straightaway.

I let out a shuddering breath. "What have they done to you?"

One side of his face has a deep purple bruise flowering below the eye and his lip has a long gash with dried blood clots all along it.

"What happened?" A fire of fury burns in my chest and I fight back angry tears. I want to touch his eye, make it better.

"Asha," he murmurs, keeping his eyes low. "You're safe!"

"What did they do to you?" He looks so battered it makes me insane with anger.

"They . . . pushed me around." His voice is quiet, flat.

I follow his gaze toward the guards. "They threw me against the wall."

"Oh, Jeevan, I'm so sorry." I risk touching the bruise lightly. "I'm going to get us out."

"How are you going to do that?"

"I . . . I don't know yet, but we'll do it somehow . . . We'll do it together." I feel for the sharp bit of metal I hid in my pocket, glance up, and keep picking at the trash. Jeevan's face looks so painful. "Does it still hurt?"

"It's not too bad." He can barely move his lips.

I know he's not telling me the truth. His hair has come undone and hangs around his shoulders; his shirt is bloodstained and torn.

I pause and press my pendant to my chest, close my eyes for a moment, try to connect with my ancestors . . . and then I feel the rhythm . . .

Asha, my dear girl. Do you remember what I told you about being special? There is a reason for everything and even though it may not seem fair that you are here, it was your destiny to come . . . Even in the vilest of places there is beauty, and it is your task to find it. Remember that I was always by your side, even when you were too small to know, and I sang to you and loved you.

The vision disappears quickly but it gives me a boost and I move closer to Jeevan. "We've got to at least *try* to get out," I say. "We can't just give up."

He shrugs and looks away, but not before I see the defeat in his eyes.

We work all day until my hands, blackened from touching the dirt and trash, are scratched all over, until the sun hovers overhead and burns an orange hole in the gray sky, and all I know is that I must think clearly. I must make a plan to get away from here and find Papa.

A shrill siren sound fills the air and suddenly everyone stops working. A crowd of children surges forward, pushing and shoving each other, shouting to get ahead.

My feet are barely touching the ground as we get carried along with the others toward a barrel of water at the foot of the mound.

A boy elbows Jeevan hard in the ribs. "That's my spot, newbie," he yells, shoving himself in front. "And *you*—get out of my spot, both of you." He glares at us.

I pull Jeevan back. "Just leave us alone."

"Yeah, leave them alone, Taran," says a skinny boy

wearing a filthy T-shirt and tattered shorts. He turns to us. "My name's Samir. Don't pay any attention to him." He forces a smile. "My friends call me Sami . . . and this is Attica."

A girl who reminds me of Roopa pushes forward. "Hi," she whispers.

"But you're too young to be here," I say.

Attica wipes her nose with the back of her hand. "I used to live with my uncle but he lost his job and said he couldn't afford to keep me anymore, so he sold me . . . That's how I ended up here."

"Sold you?" I can't believe what she's saying—but I guess that's what happened to us, isn't it? The lady in the car exchanged us for money.

"I don't think I'll ever get out," she replies, her voice on the edge of tears.

"But I look out for you, don't I?" says Sami, putting an arm around her shoulder.

"Yes," she says. "We look after each other . . . It's the only way."

We move along the line for water, all the children jostling and grabbing each other.

"Keep going," cries one of the men, stomping up and down, using a long stick to jab anyone who takes more than a few gulps of water.

I push Jeevan forward. "You go first. You've been working for longer than me."

He doesn't even bother to argue. He finishes quickly and gives me the cup, and I pour the water into my mouth. I'm so thirsty I don't want to stop, but I barely start the first sip before the man pushes me away.

"Hey," he says, "what are you, an elephant? Get back to picking . . . useless mongrels!" He snatches the drink away.

I clench my jaw as we walk back to the mound of trash and carry on picking things off the ground.

We're not allowed to stop or rest; we keep looking for wires, cans, anything metal from the dump, and stuff it into the sacks on our backs.

The sun disappears behind the tower blocks and the gray sky starts to darken. There'll be no moon tonight, and I remember how each Divali we celebrate at home is always on a moonless night. We still have four weeks. A pair of flickering floodlights turn on, and I realize we'll be working for hours yet.

A few hours later, I brush myself off, wipe the sludge off a tin, and examine it closely in the semidarkness. "Jeevan, look," I whisper.

"What are you going on about?" says Jeevan, looking confused. "We've got more important things to worry about than some silly old tin."

"No, Jeevan." I shove it under his nose. "There's a lamagaia on it." I think of Nanijee straightaway, convinced that I was *meant* to find it. "It says 'Himalayan Tea.' Maybe it's from one of those plantations near Galapoor and it's been sent as a sign to keep us strong."

Jeevan pushes the hair off his eyes to get a better look. "That *is* quite a coincidence . . . I think you could be right." He sounds animated, and for the first time he might *actually* believe it's a sign.

I slip the tin into my pocket and think of the spirit bird that watched over our journey, feel for Nanijee's pendant, and plead for it to keep me strong . . . I *will* find Papa in time and won't let anything stop me from getting out of here.

CHAPTER

28

Just when I think they're going to make us work all through the night, the high-pitched siren wails again, and everyone finally stops. My back aches and my legs feel like they might give way as we shuffle toward the crumbling old building where I spent the night.

My arms are so weak that I can barely lift them but I'm not giving in—I have to get out and find Papa. We have to make a plan.

The guards herd us like cattle through a dimly lit corridor, and I try to count how many of us there are . . . around fifty, I think. Right at the end they push us into a room reeking of soiled, damp bedding and lit by a gloomy, bare light bulb, and they lock us in.

The room is just slightly bigger than our cowshed at home and has steps leading up to a platform to make another floor, so they can squeeze everyone in.

"Over here," says Jeevan, shoving past the crowd of bodies in the semidarkness, stepping over the children too tired to move. "Let's sit next to Attica and Sami."

Suddenly the door swings open. Someone throws in a tray full of rotia, drops a container of water onto the floor, turns the heavy lock, and leaves.

Everyone rushes over to the food, pushing and shoving others out of the way. Jeevan joins in, elbowing his way to the tray.

"Here, I got a few," he says, fighting his way back through the scrum. "They're a bit stale but at least it's food."

"It's everyone for themselves here, isn't it?" I say, taking the hard bread from him.

I get the shriveled mango seedling out of my pocket and examine it. I gently trickle some water onto it, close my eyes, and say a silent prayer, willing it to recover.

"Look!" I show it to Jeevan. "It's getting better already. There's a new shoot if you look closely."

"Where? I can't see anything."

"Jeevan, you have to believe in things if you want them to happen." I put the seedling back in my pocket. We sit with our backs against the wall, dipping roti into a cup of water to soften it. The other children are a tangle of jutting ribs and filth-streaked hair, grabbing at each other, trying to get a bit more food. Attica and Sami smell terrible, and their cheeks are hollow and sunken... This is what will happen to us if we don't get out.

"I'm not staying here," I say, a growl throbbing in my throat.

Neither Sami nor Attica speaks, they just look at each other.

Attica retrieves a stub of candle and a small box of matches from behind a loose brick in the wall and lights the candle. The others in the room fall silent and, out of curiosity, I suppose, gradually gather around us.

"Has anyone ever tried to get out?" I ask. They still don't say anything. "Well, have they?"

Sami speaks first. "Don't think about it. You can't get out of here. They lock us up and keep us in order with the whips . . . and worse."

I look at Jeevan and imagine the beating he must have taken. "They don't have a right to keep any of us here," I say. "If we work together we could do it."

"Asha." It's Attica who speaks this time. "You probably think we're cowards, but we were all like you in the beginning . . . We think Sami's been here longest but there's no way of telling and every day is like the next. If you make any trouble, they just get rid of you."

"I can remember most of you arriving, *and* the ones who disappeared," says Sami. "There are plenty of children on the streets who will trust someone with the promise of a warm bed and food . . . You came, didn't you?"

"Asha didn't want to—" starts Jeevan.

I interrupt him. "Yes . . . You're right, Sami, we did, but we don't have to stay."

"There are a few hidden holes under the high wall," says Attica, taking a bite of roti and looking at Sami and the others. "A while ago a group of kids decided to make a run for it. They watched the routine of the guards and then one day they tried, while we had water break."

"They got caught," says Sami. "The guards lined them up in the sun, tied them to posts, beat them, and left them for us all to see. Then one evening they loaded them onto the dump truck...We don't know what happened after that."

Attica wipes tears with the back of her hand. "So you see, nobody will risk that again. We just do what we're told and try to keep out of their way."

I speak in a low, strong voice, and everyone's listening. I stand up to face them. "I know you're all scared and *I* am too, but sometimes you have to act together. My friend Jeevan and I have traveled all the way from our village in the foothills of the Himalayas to find my papa in Zandapur."

"And we went to the highest temple in the world," says Jeevan, "and lit deevay for all our friends and family...If you listen to Asha we might have a chance."

"It's too risky," says a boy in the crowd of faces.

"You can try if you like, but I don't want to be tied to

a post and beaten," says another. "Anyway . . . they're all in on it. Haven't you seen the police coming in for their cut? There's nowhere to go for help."

"So we have to help ourselves! You need to start realizing how long you've all been here. Look at the sky—every night the moon changes. It can tell you how the time passes if only you'll notice it. There's no moon tonight, but tomorrow it'll be like a tiny nail print and in seven days it'll be quarter. Do you really want *them* to decide your future, treat you worse than animals day after day, and get rid of you when you can't work anymore?"

Nobody answers.

"So, what do you think?" asks Jeevan.

"Yes, maybe," says Sami. But he doesn't look convinced.

"What makes her so special?" says Taran, scowling. "Why should we listen to what *she* says?"

I slump down beside Jeevan. Suddenly my doubts of the night before have come flooding back—it's hard to be hopeful in a place like this. "Taran's right," I say, the fight slipping away from me. "Why should they trust me? All I've done is put you in danger."

"You can't give up, Asha . . . not now." Jeevan makes me look at him. "Like you keep telling me, if you really want something you have to make it happen . . . We have to try at least." Suddenly he stands tall, facing the crowd of children, while I cower farther into the corner.

"Th-there's something else you should all know." Jeevan throws me a glance and gets onto an upturned water bucket. He waits until they're all looking at him, raising his hands to stop the noise. "Asha has special powers. She dreams what's going to happen . . . This journey was written in her lines . . . She feels the spirit of her nanijee."

"None of us believes in spirits, do we?" cries Taran, looking around at the others.

Everyone shouts at once, causing a huge uproar, some kids taking Jeevan's side, others gathering around Taran.

Jeevan raises his arms. "Shhh . . . Quiet, everyone. Come on, Asha, tell them."

I can't believe how Jeevan's changed his mind, but it's come too late and I sink further into my misery.

"No." I turn away from everyone, bury my head into my knees. "I can't do any more," I say, tears streaming down my face.

"I won't let you give up," says Jeevan, putting an arm around my shoulder.

I shrug him off. "You heard them. How can I make them listen when they've lost all hope . . . when *I've* lost all hope." I think of home and crumple a little bit more. I'm never going to see it again.

"Asha, come on, remember what you told me about the spirit bird . . . the things you saw in Chitragupta's house . . . I know you believe them. They're the things that make you different . . . make you strong. Asha, please, I need you—*they* need you. Think of your papa, your family."

I cautiously lift my head, wipe my nose on my sleeve, and begin to stand up. I feel like an emptied husk of wheat, my trembling insides threatening to cave in.

Jeevan heaves the bucket across and stands on it again. "Listen," he shouts above the noise. "You have a choice: You can stay here and suffer forever, or you can try to escape. Asha, tell them."

As the room gets quieter, their eyes turn to me.

"They're waiting," Jeevan says.

I nervously pull at my clothes, twisting my hands together.

"She's gone all shy," laughs Taran. "She's only a normal girl, after all. I've had enough of this."

He sparks my anger and I feel it rising like an unleashed tiger after its prey. "And *he's* only an idiot," I blurt out. "Listen to me, everyone. If we all act together we can be strong—think about your ancestors, call on their spirits to help us."

"The feather," whispers Jeevan, nudging me. "Show them the feather that links you to the lamagaia."

I clasp the long golden feather from my pocket and lift it high in the air. "This feather is from the reincarnated spirit of my nanijee—she lives on in the form of a lamagaia and she gave it to me as a sign. I also went to see the village witch, Chitragupta, and in her house I saw tigers and a whole jungle appeared to me. She showed me the things I'd only seen in my dreams." As I revisit my memories of that powerful night, I begin to feel more certain. "She gave me the confidence to believe in myself . . . She told me that I have magical powers and that I should use them for good. She said I would know when the time was right." Jeevan hands me a piece of string and I tie the feather to my arm.

He and I stand side by side like warriors, waiting for the signal to fight. I jut out my chin and feel a steely strength rebuilding inside me. Some of the children start talking among themselves, getting louder as they quibble and snipe at each other, but we stay firm.

Sami stands up. "Shhh . . ." he calls. "Let's have a vote . . . Hands up if you want this to end and to try to get out."

At first only a few of the other children put up their hands, but slowly the room becomes a sea of fingers.

CHAPTER

29

For three torturous weeks we've been imprisoned in the dump, but every night when they lock us in with spiders as large as my palm and black rats that swarm every inch of floor, we hone our escape plan.

Jeevan keeps chipping away, rallying the kids who are too scared, until only a few say it's too risky.

It's taken hours of surreptitious observation of the guards and how they operate to get all the information we need, but the resulting plan is actually quite simple. Nevertheless, we've been through it over and over again, until we can all say it by heart: When the dump truck comes around at about five p.m. to collect the scrap metal, we'll watch for when the driver gets out to help with the loading. Jeevan knows how to drive because of the tractors back home, so he's going to jump in the driving seat. The rest of us will pile into the back. There are loads of us and only a few adults—and they won't be expecting this. We should be able to do it. We've been watching the driver punch in the code for the gate and we've memorized it, so we're all set.

Last night we all watched the waning moon in the sky, ticking toward half, meaning it's just over a week until Divali—until Meena comes for her money. But we're ready for action, ready to escape. I still have time to find Papa and get home before Meena takes it.

I wake early, and as the gray light seeps through the small windows I think about the danger I'm putting everyone in. But we have to get out; otherwise we'll die here. I hold my pendant, feel my courage rising, and prepare myself for the battle ahead.

"Wake up, everyone," I yell, fire whipping through my blood. "We need to go over things one last time, so we're all absolutely sure what we're going to do today."

The bodies writhe and stir like they're part of some mythical creature with hundreds of stretching arms and legs.

I shake Attica awake. She yawns and rubs the sleep from her eyes.

"Come on, everyone . . . Get ready," says Jeevan.

"What happens if it goes wrong?" says Taran, looking toward the door. "They'll treat us worse than ever."

"It won't go wrong," says Jeevan, standing tall. "We stick to the plan, we stick together." He looks over to me. "All for one and one for all!"

"Jeevan's right." I think about Ma and Papa, Rohan and Roopa, and Jeevan. I stand on the water bucket, speaking in a loud whisper. "We'll do it together. I'm feeling stronger than ever today . . . Each night when they shove us in here, I hold my pendant and I get a sign that tells me my nanijee is listening. Don't be scared. We're going to get out." As I speak, a rush of red-hot anger pumps through me. "They have *no* right to keep us here, and today we're going to show them our power."

I lower my voice. "Don't be scared—we'll do it today.

My ma taught me to believe in myself, and together we can fight this."

Jeevan is looking so tired and thin and although his old bruises have healed, I know he's got fresh marks on his back from the guards' whips, and I feel even angrier.

The key turns in the lock. "Get up, scum," shouts one of the men.

Everyone quiets down, huddling close together, and we file out into the dump, just like we do every day, silently, eyes to the ground, but inside I know we all have a burning flame, and when the time comes it will spark into an almighty fire, sending a rush of furnace-hot anger all over the junkyard.

As we approach the towering mound of trash my eye is drawn to shadowy gray shapes high in the sky.

Lamagaias! Dozens of them!

"Look, everyone," I whisper, amazed. "Look, up there, look how many there are!"

The other children hold their arms across their foreheads, squinting to get a better look. "Wow!" they all cry . . . even Taran.

"That's incredible," says Jeevan, smiling and squeezing my arm.

They spread their wings, circling lower and lower, coming down to land on the high brick wall with razor wire across the top. When they take off again, the sun bathes their wings in golden light and they fly toward me, hovering right above, casting an immense shadow like a gigantic storm cloud over the entire mound.

"It's like a solar eclipse," says Jeevan, as if he can't believe what he's seeing.

The guards stare up, keeping their distance from us, mumbling prayers, pointing at the bronze cloud of birds.

One of the birds swoops down, landing right next to me, just like it did the first time in our garden in Moormanali.

"Nanijee!" I say. "I know it's you." I stretch my hand toward the tips of the bird's vast wings and for the very first time I touch it. A wave of power like static electricity shoots down my arm, making it tingle and shiver. Even though I was scared before, all I feel now is closeness, awakening a memory from a long time ago.

"It *is* you, isn't it? You watched over Jeevan in the forest, and made me strong enough to help him, and you've come now because I've been calling you."

She stays by my heels while the other birds gather in the sky, forming a wide circle all around the perimeter of the yard.

I clutch my pendant and study them, feeling the rhythm, which is stronger than all the times before, filling me with new hope and confidence.

My nanijee beats her wings, resting one gently on my shoulder, making me feel just like Durga, a warrior princess from the mountain kingdoms ready to fight the demons!

"That's the most amazing thing I've ever seen," says Taran, shifting his gaze. "I—I'm sorry I ever doubted you."

With a tremendous rush of air, my nanijee glides off my shoulders and joins the other lamagaias hovering in the sky.

CHAPTER

30

All day long the lamagaias circle the dump as if *they're* the guards now, sometimes flying higher, sometimes lower, but always visible.

We keep our heads down, quietly discussing the plan through the water breaks.

For a change, the guards keep well away from us, their usual taunts and violence buried in their confusion and unease over the birds circling above.

"The sun's going down," I say to Jeevan and the others. "Tell everyone that it's nearly time for the collection truck."

The message is relayed, like whispers in class, until it

ripples over the entire dump, reaching all the children.

Dark silvered clouds are gathering overhead and the sun disappears behind one of the tall buildings. I scan the circle of hovering birds, searching for my nanijee, and feel a strange sensation, as if I'm up there too, watching myself.

Nanijee, please help me if you can.

I grip my pendant, feeling the rhythm surge through my body like a thunderbolt, my heart racing, the charge of electricity filling the air.

The sky darkens, crackling with thunder, and lightning streaks across the clouds, filling the air with a tremendous noise, making everyone—including the guards—stop what they are doing and stare.

"What is it, Asha?" asks Attica, pulling at her thin dress to stop it flapping about.

I shield my eyes from the flying dust. "Don't worry," I shout to them all. "It's going to be fine."

The wind begins to blow more fiercely, gathering speed, sending loose paper wrappers and pieces of plastic shooting high into the air. Everyone's clothes stick to their thin bodies, hair whipping around their faces.

Am I making this happen?

I put my arms around Attica, protecting her from the spiraling trash, and feel the red-hot rage deep inside me . . . How did the guards get away with treating them like this for so long? Just like the men on the train, they think they can push us around, they think children have no power.

They're wrong!

I gather all my strength, every drop of misery and stifled scream, and bellow at the top of my lungs, "We're going to pay you back. Whatever happens now, we're leaving. We're not scared of you anymore." The words pour out of my mouth like boiling lava. They roar out of me in an explosive war cry.

The lamagaias continue to circle above us, their wings flashing golden against the silver gray of the billowing rain clouds, and Nanijee leaves the circle, swooping down and landing close beside me. She raises herself up as if standing on her claws, puffing her chest, making herself as tall as my waist, and I feel I could climb onto her back, ride into the skies like the goddesses from the ancient texts, breathing fire and ferocity.

"What's happening?" screams one of the guards.

"Look," says Attica. "It's the truck."

The gates fling open, the driver skids to a halt and gets out, looking at the scene in disbelief. It's the perfect distraction.

Jeevan runs toward the truck, with Sami, Attica, and the rest of us following as fast as we can.

The driver notices what's happening and grabs hold of Jeevan just as he's climbing into the driving seat.

"Let him go!" I shout, sprinting toward the driver.

But before I reach him, the spirit bird swoops down and lands on the driver's head, scratching and clawing at his hair. He screams, tumbling to the ground, struggling to get the gigantic bird off.

We cover our ears as thunder roars and lightning flashes across the sky and my nanijee rises again to join the other lamagaias.

"Look!" shouts Sami. "The metal on the dump looks like gold in the sunlight!" His voice echoes through the air. *Gold in the sunlight . . .*

"Gold!" one of the men shouts. The others turn from us and scramble on their knees, digging into the trash with their hands, stuffing whatever they can into their pockets.

"They've gone crazy," says Sami, staring at them.

I try to gather my own wits. "Quick, everyone—climb in the back of the truck."

Everyone piles in, one on top of the other, squeezing to make sure there's enough space.

"Sami, Attica, get in the passenger side," I shout, leaping in next to them.

Jeevan turns the key, pressing the accelerator, making the truck leap forward.

"Let's go," I say.

Jeevan pushes his foot down, but the truck judders to a halt and stops. It's stalled.

"The driver's coming," cries Attica, looking around.

Jeevan twists the key again, trying to get the screeching engine started.

The driver runs up to the stationary truck, trying to grab my arm through the open window as rain lashes down on him.

"Get off," I cry, my throat raw. "Quick, Jeevan." I push hard on the handle to close the window, almost trapping the driver's hand. "Start it again."

"You can't get out," yells the driver, banging on the window, rain streaming down his face. "The code's changed." He twists the handle, trying to open the door.

"Come on, Jeevan," I say desperately.

He twists the key again, stretching his legs toward the pedals.

"They're coming!" Sami cries—and he's right. The other men have regained their senses and are rushing toward us.

Suddenly, the truck starts moving and jerks toward the gate—but they catch up with us anyway, banging the sides with rocks and batons.

The birds swoop onto them, making the most ear-piercing noise, scratching at their eyes, swarming them with their immense wings, bombing them from all sides as the thunder and lightning reach a crescendo.

"Drive as fast as you can!" I cry. "It doesn't matter if the code's changed—we'll smash through the gate if we pick up enough speed."

"Look at that," says Attica.

A halo of lightning the size of the whole dump flashes above it, hitting the razor wire above the wall with a bloodcurdling bang.

"You were amazing, Asha," cries Jeevan. "You did it!"

"Put your foot down," I yell, looking back. "They're piling into a car . . . They're following us!"

CHAPTER

31

The gate splinters into pieces as we ram through it.

"Faster," I shout above the noise of the traffic. In the side mirror I can see the lamagaias still following, swooping low in front of the windshield of the pursuing car and landing on its roof. The car zigzags from one side of the road to the other, weaving behind us.

Crowds of people stand at the roadside, pointing and gaping.

Jeevan's teeth are clenched, the knuckles on his hands white from gripping the steering wheel.

"Watch out!" I cry.

He swerves, just missing a cart loaded with marigolds as the owner looks on in shock.

A huge cheer rings out from the back.

The wind is so frantic now it's practically a hurricane. The trees are bent, tossing backward and forward, branches cracking. A deafening bang shakes the road as another almighty crack of lightning hits a tree, bringing it down just behind us, blocking the road.

"Go, Jeevan," I yell until I think my lungs will burst.

There are whoops and cries from the back. "Yeah . . . GO, Jeevan!"

I glance in the rearview mirror and see the car that's following us swerve to miss the tree, but it's going too fast and smashes into it with a metallic crunch.

Sami bangs on the roof of the truck as if it's a drum . . . A massive victory cry explodes from the others.

"I told you we'd do it." I punch the air, a smile spreading across my face.

Sami looks over at Jeevan. "Where did you learn to drive like a racing star?"

Jeevan's mouth curls into a little smile and he bashes

the horn before concentrating on the road again. He looks straight ahead, crossing through traffic lights flashing green and orange, carrying on and on through what seems like the whole of the huge city.

"Look at the birds," shouts Jeevan as we exchange a quick look. "One of them is Asha's nanijee, you know."

I feel my cheeks turn hot; at last Jeevan finally believes in the power of the ancestors, and more importantly, believes in me.

The birds form a line above us and we wave at them before they rise farther into the rain-darkened sky, disappearing into the clouds.

The storm gradually subsides and the littered streets become quieter, with fewer people and less traffic.

"Jeevan, you were incredible," I say. "You just kept going!"

I pull the mango seedling from my pocket and wave it under his nose.

"I can't look now," he says. "I'm driving!"

"Well, the shoot's as long as two of my little fingers . . . *and* it's got two bright shiny new leaves growing."

"You didn't give up with your watering, even in there."

"And Jeevan, look—there's the very start of the tiniest bud appearing."

"I'm sure you'll get a mango growing before long!"

Attica wraps her arms around me. "That was like a miracle, Asha."

I put the seedling back safely in my pocket. "See what happens when we all work together?" I stroke Attica's hair, thick with dirt and full of knots, swallowing the lump in my throat. "I've got a little sister back home . . . She's just like you. Her name's Roopa."

She snuggles closer and my whole being aches for home.

"We'd better make sure we get far enough away," says Sami. "We don't want them tracking us down."

"Yeah . . . Keep going," I say.

"We should report them," says Jeevan angrily. "So they get closed down and put in prison."

"Taran already told you," says Sami. "The police take bribes . . . There's no point."

"But there must be somewhere safe . . . Not all adults are like those crooks," I say.

"There was a place where I used to live," says Sami,

his eyes lighting up. "It was for street kids ... like us. That was before they grabbed me in the market."

"Can you remember where it was?" asks Jeevan.

Suddenly the truck starts making a spluttering sound, slowing down and jolting to a standstill. There's a huge uproar from the back.

Jeevan bangs the dashboard. "Oh no! It's run out of fuel!"

"We'll just have to walk," I say. "It's fine." We climb out of the truck. "Don't worry, everyone—we're miles away from the dump now and we're going to find this shelter for street kids that Sami knows about."

Taran shuffles through the crowd of children.

"Sorry I didn't believe we could do it," he says. "We showed them though, didn't we?"

"Sami," says Jeevan, "lead the way. We need to find this place before it gets dark."

"It's been so long ... I ... I don't know if I'll remember."

"You can do it, Sami." Attica slips her hand in his. "We all worked together to escape, so finding the place won't be so hard."

"Taran," says Jeevan, taking charge, "you go right at the end; I'll go in the middle; and Sami, Asha, and Attica can go in front . . . Stick together, everyone . . . We don't want to lose anyone after coming this far."

Seeing Jeevan in control and full of enthusiasm makes my heart sing. I flash him a smile, take my place beside Sami, and grab Attica's hand. We make a line and follow Sami through the streets, past shops and high-rise buildings.

We snake through the edge of a park with trees waving feathery branches in the breeze. "I . . . I really recognize this," says Sami, slowing down. "I'm pretty sure the street shelter is on the other side of the park. I remember on Sundays they used to bring us to play kabadi here . . . Come on!"

We pick up speed, everyone chatting with excitement, almost running to keep up with Sami as he strides ahead.

He stops in front of a redbrick building with gates and a high wall around it and a buzzer to one side. A huge sign above the gate reads:

ZANDAPUR SHELTER—
HOME FOR STREET CHILDREN

"This is it," says Sami, his voice trembling.

"But we're not coming with you," I say. "Our journey doesn't end yet . . . I have to find Papa."

Attica grabs my sleeve. "You've been like my sister."

I give her a huge squeeze. "Take care, won't you?"

"We hope you find him," says Taran.

"Look at the moon and think of me . . . I'll be watching it too, far off in Moormanali in the foothills of the Himalayas."

All the children surround us, pushing to say goodbye. They circle Jeevan, patting him on the back, and begin chanting, "Jeevan . . . Jeevan . . . Jeevan."

"You were incredible," say Sami and Taran at the same time.

He puts an arm around the boys, his face glowing, his smile the widest I've seen in ages. "Anytime."

Sami and Taran gather all the children.

"I'll ring the buzzer. They were really kind—don't be frightened, anyone," Sami says.

A large smiley woman bustles out of the street shelter. "What's all this noise? Children . . . What's happening here?" She comes closer to Sami, peering at him from behind the bars of the gate. "No! Can it be? Little Samir?" She unlocks the gate, clasping Sami's face in her hands. "What happened to you? So long . . ."

Sami brushes a tear with the back of his hand. "It *is* me, Auntie Lakshmi."

She pulls him toward her, wrapping her arms around him, kissing him all over. "Come inside . . . Wait till the others see you! Dev, Puja—quick, come here!" she calls out, and two people run out of the building toward us. "*And* your friends . . . Come off the street, all of you."

"Quick, Jeevan," I whisper. "Before she scoops us up too!" I duck and shuffle back onto the street, mingling farther into the crowd of children, pulling Jeevan along with me.

CHAPTER
32

We stand outside the street shelter, a fierce pride blooming in my chest when I think of everything we've gotten through together.

I link arms with Jeevan, and when I shoot him a glance the feeling fades as quickly as a blown-out candle flame. I've put him through so much: His clothes are torn, his hair is gray from the dust and dirt of the dump, his hands are covered in cuts and bruises. If his ma could see him now she'd hardly recognize him. She always used to make sure his clothes were washed and ironed.

"I'm sorry," I say, my voice small and gruff.

"We'll find your papa." He takes my hand. "You're strong, Asha. Look what we did. We'll find him and the three of us will go home together."

Maybe if his ma saw him now, with that fearless look on his face, she wouldn't be able to help but be proud.

Darkness is creeping into the sky, and even though it isn't cold, a shiver trembles down my spine as we turn away from the street shelter and think about venturing back into Zandapur.

"I found some rupees in the truck. Why don't we get a rickshaw?" asks Jeevan, sticking out his arm. "Look at that one!"

A motor rickshaw strung with glowing rainbow lights is slowing down, coming toward the street shelter.

"Remember what happened the last time we got a taxi?" I say. "But we don't have much choice . . . wander alone in Zandapur or take another risk."

"And you never know," he says, "they might come prowling for us . . . Anyway, how else will we find Connaught Place at night?"

A singsong voice springs out of the rickshaw. "Connaught Place?" asks the driver, stepping out and yawning. "I was just finishing my shift and about to go home . . . but jump in and Raj will be happy to take you to your destination." He looks at us with sad eyes.

His rickshaw could win a prize for the most colorful vehicle in the whole of the city, with its painted palm trees, golden sunsets, and elephants. Piled high on the roof and stuffed into every window are the most beautiful cushions I've ever seen. Even in the semidarkness the colors are electric. There are green-and-red ones, swirled ones, and striped ones.

"After what we've been through, I don't know if we should," I whisper to Jeevan, my heart beating hard. "Let's think about it for a minute." I run my fingers through my hair and try to brush some dirt out. My clothes are stiff with filth and we must both smell awful.

"H-how do we know you won't take us somewhere else?" I ask.

He looks serious. "There are many bad people in the city—I am not one of those, I promise." He begins to get back into his rickshaw. "It's your choice . . . only if you want a safe rickshaw." He opens his wallet and shows us a photo. "This is my daughter . . . and this is Lakshmi, my wife . . . and who's this handsome fellow? Oh. It's me," he chuckles.

He sits at the wheel of his taxi and speaks to us through the window. "My wife makes cushions," he says. "I deliver them around the city." He looks in his mirror and makes a funny face as if he's thinking. "I have a special big assignment." He twists around. "You see the cushions? Big wedding, big cushion order." And then he speaks more quietly. "Royal wedding. Hush hush. Palace at the edge of the city. Beautiful cushions for beautiful princess and guests' big bottoms."

I've almost forgotten what it feels like to laugh, and I can't help the giggles exploding . . . but the next minute I'm smearing dirty tears across my face. "W-we were trapped in a dump," I blurt.

He gets out of the taxi again and smiles. "Squish in—Raj will take you. No more crying . . . OK?" He dabs at my cheeks with the cuff of his shirt. "Bit better, little one? You look like you have suffered enough . . . Would make my Lakshmi cry too."

"W-we've come from Moormanali to find my papa."

"He lives at 102 Connaught Place," adds Jeevan.

Raj raises his eyebrows and whistles. "Long way!" He starts moving the cushions. "We'll put them in the front . . . so they don't get dirty? And—don't be offended—but maybe I put this plastic on the seats?"

I look down at my blackened fingernails and shove my hands behind my back.

"And one more thing," he says seriously. "You know anyone else who can do this?" He wiggles his ears and his eyes spin around at the same time. He ruffles Jeevan's messy hair. "You want to learn this?"

"He's funny," laughs Jeevan, copying Raj.

"I think we can trust him," I giggle. "Let's get in."

I let my shoulders slump against Jeevan and wipe my cheeks.

"We can pay."

"I'll charge you a cheap price . . . All relaxed now? Get steady and go!"

Raj zips around the busy roads beeping his horn, even though there doesn't seem to be any need. It's like he's on parade and wants everyone to look at him.

He clicks his GPS and we take a sharp turn off the main road into a smaller street, which seems to go on forever.

"Nearly there," he calls from the front. "This is where the factories are."

"I know Papa's working in a factory," I say to Jeevan. "But surely he doesn't live in one as well?"

"What these men do for their families," says Raj, twisting to talk to us. "Here is 58," says Raj, slowing the taxi down and peering at the buildings on his side of the road. "74 . . . 100 . . . Oh . . ." His voice trails off and sounds all wrong. "There it is." He slows right down and stops.

My chest thuds as if it's going to break; 102 Connaught Place is a charred husk of a building with blackened windows, which stare back at me like dark, hollow eyes. The ground in front is littered with lengths of half-burnt fabric.

Has Papa been caught in a fire? Was he trapped inside?

I fling the rickshaw door open and hurtle toward the building. "No!" I cry. "No . . . !" My voice is strangled, everything is blurred. The stinging smell of fumes clings to the air. I feel Jeevan's arms holding me, hear Raj trying to talk to me, soothing me.

I pull myself away from their grip and hurl myself on the filthy charcoal-covered ground.

"Papa!" I scream. "Papa!"

CHAPTER

33

"Papa, what's happened? Where are you?" I cover my face with my hands, tears seeping through my fingers. Raj's and Jeevan's far-off voices are dull in the background.

Jeevan puts his arm around my shoulder. "Asha."

"I know he's alive . . . I have to find him."

"We . . . We don't know," says Jeevan, moving closer to me.

I stare at the burnt-out factory in a daze, trying to figure out what to do. "But someone must know . . . They must have seen *something*." I grab hold of a passing man's sleeve. "Help me."

Raj pulls me back and holds the rickshaw door open. "Oh, betay, you poor thing. These factories are not fit for anything."

"Asha, look what I found." Jeevan leaps into the rickshaw next to me, waving a dirty piece of paper in the air. He squeezes my arm. "Look," he says, showing me the small poster. "I found this pasted to the side of the building."

Raj starts the engine. "You've had such a shock . . . I'll take you home. My wife, Lakshmi, and I can look after you." We drive back along the road, away from Connaught Place.

The paper trembles between my fingers.

Jeevan holds it steady. "It says that this charity is campaigning for better working conditions in factories, and helping the survivors of this fire . . . Look, there's an address."

"Raj can take us!" I cry.

I shout to him over the noise of the traffic, showing him the poster. "Raj, look what Jeevan found. This charity might know something about the fire . . . Do you know where it is?"

He slows the rickshaw down, and I push the poster toward him.

"Yes . . . but listen"—he gives it back to me—"it is *so* dark, *so* late . . . Come to my home. Lakshmi will look after you and then tomorrow you can find it . . . Is it an idea?"

Everything comes crashing down, the exhaustion of the brutal weeks at the dump finally ripping into my spirit. "Yes," I murmur, covering my face with my hands, tears escaping through my fingers. "Can you take us home, please?"

I can feel Jeevan's thin arm around me, but everything else is like a terrible nightmare. The inside of the taxi feels unreal, like I'm sleepwalking, with all the animals climbing off the cushions . . . Then they fade away and I can't hear or see anything other than a deep, deep darkness, like a noiseless cave in the depths of a turbulent sea.

When I wake, my clothes feel soft and smell of washing powder. Someone's changed me into pajamas and I'm tucked into a small wooden bed. Cries of parakeets squawk through an open window. As I prop myself up on my elbow I notice a fringe of green banana leaves poking into the room.

Then I drag it all back—the dump, the factory... Papa!

A rap on the door makes me jump as it springs open and a large woman dressed in a bright blue sari stands in the doorway.

"I'm Lakshmi... Raj's wife," she says, smiling. "I've brought you some fruit and something to drink." She stretches over to rearrange the covers, lifting me gently so I'm sitting upright.

"My papa!"

"Shhh," she says, putting her finger to her lips. "No need to speak."

She passes her hand over my short, clean hair and fusses over me.

"The other children have told me all about you." She spoons pieces of orange into my mouth. "And all about that disgusting junkyard."

"Th-they're all here?" I let the fruit slip down whole without tasting anything. I know that Lakshmi's only being kind but I don't want to hear any more, I just want to get out and find Papa.

Jeevan bursts into the room. "Asha . . . Raj and Lakshmi run the street shelter."

"Th-that's a-amazing!"

The doorway is crammed with the shiny faces of all our friends from the dump.

"Let Asha rest," says Lakshmi, shooing the others out of the room, but Attica squeezes through and jumps onto the bed, giving me a huge hug. "You too, Attica."

I hug her back. "Go on," I say, forcing a small smile.

Lakshmi closes the door and comes back to the bed. "More sleep, that's what you need."

"I don't want to sound ungrateful—Raj has been so kind, and you—but I have to find my papa." I grab hold of the poster from last night. "I have to find this place."

"Why don't we just call them?" says Jeevan gently.

I nod—it'll be quicker that way.

"You have to be even braver now," says Lakshmi, helping me out of bed. "Prepare yourself for what they might say."

We go next door, where the others are just finishing

breakfast. I pull up a chair and get ready to make the call, my fingers shaking as I try to carefully press the numbers, everyone watching in silence.

The fear rises inside me and however hard I try, I can't push it away. At last I'm going to find out what's happened to Papa . . . Is he alive or not?

CHAPTER
34

"What did they say?" asks Jeevan as soon as I put the phone down.

"We have to go to the hospital," I say. "They said he might be there."

I rush to the bedroom, get dressed, and collect the mango seedling, but the bud that was forming yesterday is looking a little crushed and makes me pause.

"Look what's happened to it!" I say to Jeevan, placing it on the breakfast table in the other room.

"I'm sure it will recover," he replies.

"Why don't I pot it for you?" says Lakshmi, taking it

from me. "All it needs is a bit of water...and Raj is waiting downstairs so you can get to the hospital straightaway."

"Thank you, Lakshmi," I say, my heart beating fiercely. "It might be silly, but I don't want to leave without the seedling—I've carried it all this way for my papa, you see."

The others wish us luck and, clutching tight to the seedling safely planted in a small terra-cotta pot, I sprint down the stairs with Jeevan at my side. We rush through the courtyard and jump into Raj's taxi with Lakshmi following behind.

"Good morning, little sir and madam," says Raj, starting up the rickshaw. "What lovely perfume you wear today...No worrying, OK? All will turn good."

Raj drops us in front of the enormous hospital building, which looms ominously in the middle of its sprawling gardens, and I'm weak with fear. The thoughts I've been trying to quiet are now screaming in my head: What if he's not here after all, or what if he's so badly hurt he'll never be the same again?

It feels like snakes are crawling through my stomach

as I push open the wide glass doors and rush ahead of Jeevan and Lakshmi toward the reception desk. As Jeevan catches up with me, I slow down, dragging my feet, almost wanting to turn back. "I'm scared, Jeevan," I whisper.

"We don't know anything for sure yet," says Jeevan, touching my arm. "And I know that's hard . . . But the one thing that has kept you strong is your hope and what you believe." He takes my hand and together we stand before the desk.

Tugging at my sleeves, I take a deep breath, hold my pendant for courage, and feel its rhythm pulse through me. "I'm looking for my papa," I say. "He was in the factory fire at Connaught Place."

A nurse looks up from behind the reception desk, giving me a hard stare.

I tug at the ratty ends of hair that barely cover my neck and pass my hand over the rest, trying to smooth it down.

"Yes . . . We do have a few men from that fire here."

"We are all together," says Lakshmi, hurrying along.

My heart gives a huge twist as I stand on tiptoes, peering over the desk.

"But I'm afraid the papers of all those men were destroyed in the fire, so we don't have any names." The nurse puts her pen down and stands up.

I swallow. "Please . . . I have to find him. My ma is back in our village. I've come from Moormanali."

"But that's hundreds of miles." She raises her eyebrows. "Let me see if I can find someone . . . We're very busy." She waves her hand to another nurse. "Nurse Marler will take you, my dear." She gives a tired smile, then carries on with her work.

We follow Nurse Marler as she clips along the white-tiled corridor.

"Try not to worry," says Jeevan.

"Try not to worry? Are you crazy?" My insides are like springs, tightening and unraveling with each step. "I didn't mean to snap like that. I'm sorry, Jeevan."

Lakshmi strokes my cheek and we carry on down the long corridor.

When at last we arrive at the ward, sweat drips slowly down my back as I stare along the line of beds, crammed closely together. Long twisted wires filled with glistening liquid are attached to each patient's arm, sending shivers spiraling down my spine.

"This is where most of the men are," says the nurse kindly. "Don't be shocked . . . We'll go along the beds, see if you can find your papa."

"I'll stay right by you whatever happens, Asha," says Jeevan.

"I wouldn't be able to do this without you, you know."

Moving slowly along the row, I scan each face. As I approach each new person, my heart almost leaps into my mouth; perhaps the next one will be Papa, no, the next one has to be him . . . But none of them are and then the beds come to an end.

"My papa's not here." I sway, suddenly feeling hot as sourness rises into my throat. "I'm going to be sick." I cling to Jeevan.

"You need some fresh air," says Lakshmi, scooping her arm around my back.

"Here, quick." The nurse scrapes a chair toward me. "Oh, honey . . . I'm so sorry."

Lakshmi takes out a folded handkerchief and a bottle of water from her bag. She wets the handkerchief and dabs my face.

Jeevan fans me with a piece of folded paper.

I stare up at them all, still feeling queasy.

"I don't want to get your hopes up," says the nurse, "but there *is* one last room." She pats my hand. "A small one on the left over there, with a man who keeps shouting in his sleep, disturbing the others. That's why he's in the room by himself."

I struggle to my feet. "What if it's not him?"

"We won't know until we go and look," says Jeevan. "We've got one more chance."

The sweet scent of jasmine blows in through an open window, filling me with memories of home, of Ma, Roopa and Rohan, Moormanali.

The nurse shows us to the room and I try to control my racing heart.

"I'll wait out here," says Lakshmi.

I push the handle down and creak the door open. Even with Jeevan right beside me, I hesitate before walking in.

The bandaged figure on the bed faces away from me. All I can see are a pair of scarred hands resting on the white sheet. I put the mango seedling on the table and creep closer, moving around the bottom of the bed to get a better look.

My papa's hands were smooth and strong but these are blistered and burnt.

His eyes are squeezed closed, his cracked lips parted, he looks so old and in pain, but I'd know that face anywhere!

"Papa! I've found you . . . at last!"

I throw my arms around his thin body, resting my head lightly on his chest. My tears drip onto the woolen blanket, slowly at first, then spilling out as fast as the Ganges.

"What happened to you, Papa?" I touch the bandage on his forehead, but he doesn't open his eyes, and fear flashes through me.

"Asha! You found him!" Jeevan flings his arm around my shoulder.

I lean into him. "*We* found him."

The nurse rushes in, followed by Lakshmi.

"It *is* your papa, then?" asks the nurse.

"What wonderful news, Asha," says Lakshmi, grasping my hand.

"It is," I say, my voice trembling. "But he won't open his eyes and I don't know what's wrong with him . . . He's not like the papa I remember at all."

"We don't know exactly what happened in the factory. He was unconscious when he came in. We think he has traumatic amnesia."

"What does that mean? When will he open his eyes and recognize me? What's wrong with him?"

"It means he can't remember anything," says Jeevan, pulling his arm tighter around my shoulder.

The nurse frowns. "He couldn't tell us who he was. He must have had a fall. Because he didn't have any documents on him, nobody knew who to contact."

"But he *will* get better . . . *Won't he?*" I grasp the nurse's arm.

"Listen . . . You have to be brave. This is hard for me to tell you, especially since your ma is so far away, but I have to be honest with you—he might have permanent brain damage."

Lakshmi gives the nurse a hard stare.

Papa's breathing is even and hardly sounds like anything's wrong at all. Maybe they're mistaken and when he wakes up he'll be the same as before.

"Sorry, I know it's not what you want to hear."

My throat is tight with grief. "So he may never remember me?"

CHAPTER

35

You wouldn't believe what's happened to these children and how they've fought to get here," Lakshmi says to the nurse. "They need to stay positive."

Nurse Marler bristles. "But he's still not well, and I don't want to raise hopes only for them to be disappointed . . . The fact is, we really don't know what the long-term effects of his accident will be." She checks Papa's notes. "But now that the family has been located, it may be possible to discharge him."

"You can all stay with us for a few days before going

back," Lakshmi leaps in. "You can't travel with him like this."

"But we have to be back home by Divali." My voice is panicky. "I need to let Ma know that we've found him and we'll be home by then."

"Just a few days," Lakshmi says again. "Do you have your ma's phone number?"

"There's no signal in the village," I say.

"Maybe we can send a telegram instead? Old ways are best! Your ma will get the message on the same day and it's a week until Divali . . . plenty of time for you all to recover."

"Can I stay with him tonight?" I ask, gripping his hand tightly.

"Mmm . . ." ponders the nurse. "We usually wouldn't allow it . . . but I'll be able to twist the sister's arm, in these special circumstances."

"So it's all settled," says Lakshmi. "And I'll get Raj to drop in a few things from home for you."

"Can you bring me a deeva, please? It might help him to get better. Now that I've found him, I'm not leaving him for a minute."

Jeevan gives me a clumsy hug. "See you in the morning, Asha." He's trying to hide it but I know he's as worried as I am. "Everything's going to be fine . . . Just look at the bright green bud on the mango seedling."

A little while later there's a knock on the door and it opens slightly. "All sorted with the sister in charge." The nurse winks at me. "Your funny friend Raj dropped this off for you—honestly, he had us all in stitches—some fresh clothes, something to eat, and a few deevay, he said."

I take the bag. "Thank you."

"Be careful with the deeva though, won't you? I shouldn't really let you but you've wrapped me right around your little finger, and if it gives you a little hope . . ." Her voice trails off.

I give her my best smile in case she changes her mind.

Outside, the sun is setting, sending rays of darkest orange and purple bursting onto Papa's face, turning his pale skin the most beautiful shade of gold. "I can hardly believe I've found you, Papa," I whisper, holding his hands once the nurse has left. I remember all those times he helped me when I was ill or hurt and now it's my turn to help him.

I trace the lines on his palms, desperate to know if they show a happy ending. He shifts on the bed and his eyelids give a brief flutter, but he still doesn't wake.

I lift the mango seedling that I've carried through our whole journey and examine it. It made such a long journey in its fragile banana leaf and survived so much. Now in its fresh new pot it's starting to look like a proper little plant. I balance it on the scratched metal table next to the bed, lift the heavy water jug, and pour a few drops onto it.

Lakshmi must have given me one of her special deevay, ones she's bought specially for Divali. The clay is painted bright shiny yellow and there are tiny glass pieces all around the rim. I run my finger along the edge—it's so pretty. I carefully strike a match, light the deeva, and place it in front of the seedling.

I screw my eyes tightly closed, place my palms together, and say a prayer . . . I hear the rushing water of the Ganges, the mountain winds whistling their way through the valleys of Moormanali, and I connect to the ancient rhythms of my ancestors.

The light is fading fast, and in the growing darkness the orange flicker of the deeva lights up the mango seedling.

With fresh confidence I begin my incantation to bring Papa back from the shadowy world he has been stuck in these past months. "Papa." I bow my head with love. "The journey to find you has been so long and treacherous . . . I've had to fight my way to get here, crossing mountains, facing dangers I could only have imagined, and now I ask, if you can hear me, wake up so we can all go home. Ma is waiting all by herself with Rohan and Roopa."

I rest my head against his chest, listening to the thump-thumping of his heart. "I've come to get you, Papa. You have to remember me. It was so hard—Jeevan got really ill in the forest, then we climbed all the way to the highest temple in the world . . . Some men trapped us in a junkyard and made us work until our fingers bled. Ma borrowed money, Pa—and there's a deadline. We have to pay the loan back by Divali or we'll lose our home forever." I take Papa's hand and rest it against my cheek. A tear rolls down his finger. "That's why I need you to remember me. I need your help."

The evening ticks by and I watch Papa closely as each hour slips into the next, waiting for him to wake up.

Finally, his lashes move briefly before his eyes spring open in fright, as if he's still dreaming. He looks past me without saying a word.

"Papa, it's me . . . It's Asha." I grip the blanket more tightly.

I hold his face between my palms, turning it so he *has* to look at me. His face is blank but I'm frantic to help him remember. I take off my pendant, push it into his hand. "Look at this. It's Nanijee's necklace— the one she gave to Ma, and Ma gave it to me because it's my turn to wear it now. It helped me to be strong . . . Ma said that *I* decide what I believe for myself. That's what I did—I believed my dreams and they helped me to find you."

But he doesn't seem to see it and lets it fall from his hand.

CHAPTER
36

I press the pendant back into his palm and hold it there, as if we're sharing a prayer, feeling its rhythm as the curved shape touches our skin. I unclasp my hand and it seems to send out a glow, lighting up his face.

I lift the mango seedling and brush the leaves under his nose. "Look, Papa, I carried the stone all the way from our orchard back home."

He blinks and frowns as if the scent has reminded him of something, but the blank expression returns and he drops his head to one side.

"Please remember us."

"When is the nurse coming?" he says, ignoring me. "She comes every day."

"We have to get home to Moormanali, Papa."

"Where's that?" His voice is quiet, confused. "This is my home. Who are you? Why are you calling me Papa?"

I know he doesn't mean it, but his words hurt more than anything that's happened so far.

The song he used to sing to me comes into my head, and I sing it as softly and sweetly as I can.

"Uncle Moon's gone far away,
Where's he gone? Where's he gone?
Far, far away.
Chanda Mama dhoor ke,
Chanda Mama dhoor ke.
Kithay ke? Kithay ke?
Dhoor, dhoor ke."

The lullaby calms him to sleep as the sky outside turns midnight blue and I watch over him.

But then he opens his eyes suddenly, although he's

still asleep. "Hot, burning hot," he cries out again and again, his face filled with panic as if he's back in the factory seeing the horror over and over again.

"I'm here, Papa." I try to wake him from the nightmare. "It's all over. You're safe."

But it doesn't make any difference. He stays inside his head, locked away from me. I lie next to him, tears sliding from the corners of my eyes, and watch him fall asleep again, without knowing who I am.

What's the point? Nothing is working—not my prayers, not the mango seedling I've carried and nurtured . . . nothing! I lay my head on the blanket and, completely exhausted, let sleep wash over me.

In the morning, dawn edges its way into the small room, filling every corner with a soft pink haze as I wake slowly from an exhausting sleep.

I stare in wonder at the seedling beside the bed, which has grown overnight and now is at least as tall as my arm, with dozens of new leaves and blossoms. Its roots have spread through the bottom of the pot, covering the table in a network of fine spirals. The room fills with the scent of sweet, ripe mango, and when I look closer, hidden behind the leaves is a small oval fruit, yellow striped with red.

A tapping on the window startles me but I leap off the bed and pull aside the curtains.

"Nanijee! It's you! You came to see Papa . . ." I stretch my arms out flat against the cold window, but still her wings are way longer. I press my face so close to hers that I see her golden-flecked eyes. "But he doesn't know me, Nanijee . . . He just can't remember."

She taps three more times with her smooth gray beak.

"What can I do?"

She beats her wings, arcing high above the trees, and swoops off into the sky. I watch her until she's a tiny dot, until I can't see her anymore, but I know she's still there somewhere, that she won't be far away.

"R-Rohan?"

I rush to Papa's side and he sweeps his fingers across my head. "What are *you* doing here?"

"No, Papa," I laugh. "It's *me*, it's Asha."

He cups my face in his hands. "Asha—of course—how could I mistake you?" His voice is raspy, each word forming slowly. "I feel . . . so tired."

I fling my arms around him. "Papa . . . my papa," I cry, burrowing into the blanket. "You've been ill for a long time, but you're going to get better." The ancient rhythms sweep through me and I know that all my ancestors are with me.

"Why did you cut your beautiful hair?"

"Papa, I went to the highest temple in the world so I could find you. I cut my hair and made a sacrifice."

"I've been in a dream," he continues, still speaking carefully. "I dreamt about a fire."

"There was a fire in the factory but we didn't know why your letters stopped . . . I read your last letter over and over again."

He puts his arms around me and I curl my body against his—the moment I've waited for is finally here.

"My darling Asha."

"Jeevan and me," I say between sobs. "We came to find you together."

He pulls me closer, kissing the top of my head. "No more tears now."

The nurse pushes open the door and nearly drops the breakfast tray. "Your papa's speaking to you?" she says, putting the tray on the side table. "I can't believe it, that's incredible. I don't know what magic you did in here last night"—she smiles—"but it's definitely worked— What's that huge mango plant doing in here?"

"Does that mean we can go home?" asks Papa. "How is your ma—my beautiful Enakshi—and Rohan and Roopa?"

The nurse pushes him gently back onto the pillow. "Don't overexcite yourself—I'll still have to check with the doctor." She puts some pills into a container and hands them to Papa with a glass of water.

"We all missed you so much. Papa, we met people in Zandapur who helped us. Lakshmi and Raj." I take a big gulp of air. "A-and they say we can stay with them for a few days before we go home." I rest against the pillow, trying to catch my breath.

"I think that's enough information for the moment," says the nurse, handing Papa a small see-through bag with a dirty folded envelope inside. "It was in your pants pocket."

"Thank you, nurse," says Papa. "It's the wages I was saving to send home."

I tuck my head into Papa's shoulder. "It was hard for Ma, but she did her best . . ." I whisper.

"My . . . little Ashi." He strokes my hair.

Every time I look at him, he seems more and more like my old papa. I hold on to him as tightly as I can.

"I'm never going to let you go," I say. "Ever."

CHAPTER

37

It's early morning, and Papa and I are taking our daily stroll around the garden of the street shelter while Jeevan and the others mill about, helping to keep everything clean and tidy. Lime-green parakeets swoop through the coconut palms, whistling to each other.

Raj bustles out of the house. "Hey, Mr. Champion, look at you," he laughs. "We'd sign you up to the Zandapur Charity Run if you could stay any longer."

"I can't believe it was only a few days ago that I was still in the hospital . . . Lakshmi's been fattening me up with her amazing rice and dhal," jokes Papa.

"Well, it's definitely working!" says Raj, heading over to his rickshaw and starting to clean it.

"Are you ready for a rest now, Papa?" I ask as I unhook my arm and we sit down at the breakfast table.

"Lakshmi sent some chai and jelaybia," says Attica, carefully carrying in a small jug and pretty tea glasses on a tray. She pours the sweet chai and offers it to us.

I take a sip. "You make the best chai, Attica."

"I only helped with collecting the spices," she says, giving us a smile that reminds me of the white bakul flowers back home. "Thank you, Asha." She beams before running off to collect the eggs.

I haven't told Papa about Meena and the loan yet—not while he's been awake—but I know I should. I'm scared of worrying him, of somehow setting back his recovery. My stomach twists in case he's still not strong enough, but I grip the table and launch in. "Th-there's something important you need to know, Papa. Ma... She had to borrow some money," I blurt out.

His face tenses and he grows pale. "I... Of course. The money would have stopped. My poor Enakshi." He takes a deep breath and places his hand on my arm and I can feel it trembling. "What happened?" he asks. "Tell me everything."

"Ma borrowed the money from a woman called Meena," I say, the words catching in my throat. "She kept thinking the money to pay her back would come through, but it never did, and eventually Meena came to the farm with two men. They broke some things in the house and took the tractor. She said it was the interest payment." Papa is quiet and simply strokes my hair. It gives me the courage to tell him the rest. "She said she'd come back at Divali at night-fall for the full repayment of the loan. She'll take our home, Papa."

"It's all right, Asha. We have my wages and there's some money in my account—compensation from the fire." He looks across the garden toward the gate, nodding slowly. "The deadline's the day after tomorrow, then. *And* it's your birthday." He glances down at me fondly. "We need to get home as soon as we can. I'm so sorry this has happened. You've been so brave."

I feel warmth rising inside me. "When Ma gave me Nanijee's pendant, it connected me to our ancestors and her spirit showed me the way to you—I believe she kept watch over us in the form of a lamagaia—at every step of this long journey she's been with us. But"—I glance up at him—"are you sure you're all right to travel so soon?"

He puts his arm around me. "I think the thunder on the night you were born made you extra special. Don't worry about me, my little Ashi, I'm feeling stronger every day."

This time Papa takes *my* hand and we walk together toward the veranda, where Taran is stringing paper decorations along the ceiling. "We're going to start Divali a little early," he says with a smile. "Give you a proper send-off."

In the evening we sit down to the farewell meal, which everyone's been helping to prepare. There's a new green cloth on the table with fragrant frangipani flowers lining the middle. In the center are bowls of steaming golden dhal and on either side two large bowls of rice—one plain and the other splashed yellow with saffron.

Papa sits on one side of me, Jeevan on the other.

Sami stands on his chair and raises his glass of homemade lemonade. "To Asha and Jeevan," he says. "To the amazing spirit bird and to all of us for our incredible escape." The others all join in cheering and laughing.

"Divali Mubarak," says Raj. "Happy Divali."

I smile and join in the toast, but I'm reminded again of the deadline.

CHAPTER

38

It's late morning at Zandapur station, the day we're finally leaving for home. Our journey will be slow through the steep mountain villages but by night-fall we should have reached Galapoor. Then first thing tomorrow—the morning of Divali—we'll speed toward Sonahaar and get to Moormanali before dark.

"Look at you!" says Papa. "It was so kind of Lakshmi to make you an outfit for your birthday, and to make Jeevan a shirt."

I swoosh the ground with my lengha skirt, the magenta-colored sequins sparkling as they catch the light. A smile spreads like a half-moon right across my face when I clutch the folds of the full skirt, feeling like Sita returning from exile; the only thing missing is a golden bow. Even so, a knot of nervousness still coils in my stomach. We're going home, but will we make it in time to pay Meena off?

Papa sits down while Jeevan and I get in line for tickets. Jeevan takes my hand and squeezes it, as if he knows what's going through my mind. He looks so handsome in his new shirt—I know his ma will burst into tears when she sees him. We stand together, waiting our turn.

"Close your eyes and hold out your arm." Jeevan snaps me out of my daydream.

What's this all about? I feel his fingers tying something soft around my wrist.

"You can open them now," he says, beaming. "I know it's a day early but with everything else happening tomorrow . . . Happy birthday!"

I touch the orange-and-pink woven band. "Wow . . . Did you make it?"

"Attica helped."

"It's so pretty, my favorite colors." I kiss him lightly

on the cheek. "Thank you." My face flushes. "For everything."

He darts his eyes to the ground and nods, turning nearly as purple as my lengha.

We buy the tickets and return to Papa. I give him the change and we make our way toward the train.

A chattering murmuration of starlings perches on high wires above the platform and hordes of noisy people mill about, buying snacks and fragrant chai for the train.

"This is going to be the best birthday ever," I say, squeezing Papa's hand.

"I wish I could have gotten you something," he says, disappointment in his eyes. "Even if it was only small."

"Finding *you* was the best present ever, Papa!" I link arms with him, resting my head against the crook of his arm.

Lakshmi, Raj, Sami, and Attica emerge from the crowd and hurry toward us.

"Just one more goodbye!" Lakshmi laughs, giving us a huge hug. "We're so pleased it's all worked out."

Papa puts his hands together in thanks. "I won't

forget what you did for Asha and Jeevan . . . and me."

"Goodbye." I hug Lakshmi and then Raj, Sami, and finally Attica. I lift her up just like I do with Roopa and she winds her legs around my waist. "You have to come to Moormanali. You'll love it."

"What a great idea," says Papa. "Come for a mountain break . . . Bring all the children."

"We'll save up," says Raj.

Jeevan slaps Sami on the back. "You have to come. I promised I'd teach you to drive, didn't I?"

"We'd better get on," says Papa. "We don't want the train going without us . . . Come on, you two."

The three of us link arms and walk along the platform together, but just before we board, I turn and give our friends a final wave.

Just like with the train at Sonahaar all those weeks ago, the hot, narrow corridor is full of people jostling and shoving to get to their seats. We stop to show the tickets to a guard wearing a sky blue turban.

"Going home with your family for Divali?" he asks, sliding open a wooden compartment door and showing us inside.

"Yes," Papa replies, pulling us close.

"Have a good journey, yaar."

"We will," says Papa, smiling.

The final fringes of Zandapur flash past the window. The small, fragile houses with corrugated tin roofs stand together, while glass tower blocks reflect the white smoggy sky, and women in multicolored saris carry bricks on their heads. I think of Attica, Sami, and the others and hope they *do* come to see us one day.

Jeevan's fallen asleep leaning into the corner, where the seat meets the window. I take off my long chunni with lilac trim, fold it, and tuck it under his head.

The clackety-clack of the iron wheels makes it impossible to stay awake and I feel my eyelids closing to the rhythm of the train.

I dream of all the places I've been and all the people I've met. Of tigers, wolves, and soaring mountains, of kindly shepherds, solemn pilgrims, and devious junk-yard owners, of my mystical nanijee and the sprouting mango, all the dreams intertwined.

From time to time, I faintly hear the carriage door

slide open and closed. I'm still worried about reaching home on time, but right now, there's nothing I can do about it. The abrupt punch of the ticket machine snaps me awake once, but I sleep more deeply than I have since leaving home.

The train begins to shake, slowing down, its wheels screeching against the metal rails. I open my eyes slowly and see that Papa's already awake, and so is Jeevan.

The train enters Sonahaar station slowly, coming to a standstill at a busy platform jammed with people searching for their families.

"Come on!" says Papa. "We're here."

We collect our belongings and Papa puts his arms around us as we hurriedly leave the compartment.

"It feels strange being back here again after so long, doesn't it?" says Jeevan.

"I know," I say, pushing my way out of the crowded train.

Papa leads the way and we head out of the station toward a line of yellow taxis puffing dark fumes into the air. A cooling wind shakes the neem tree where I sheltered from the traffic six whole weeks ago, and now the first of its autumn leaves are spiraling through the air, landing in untidy piles on the ground.

Papa leads us to a bright orange rickshaw. We climb in and before we know it, we're speeding through the streets, leaving the town behind us and heading down the long straight road to Moormanali.

I remember how I made this same journey before, hidden in the cart. I don't have to hide now; it doesn't matter who sees me—I'm with my papa. I can't wait to hug Rohan and Roopa and I can hardly sit still I'm so excited to see Ma, but every time I think of her, my stomach begins to whirl.

CHAPTER

39

The rickshaw swings around a corner and bumps over the dirt road that leads to Moormanali.

"I can't take you right into the village, the road's too bad," shouts the driver over the noise of the engine. "You'll have to walk the last bit."

"We're almost there," I say to Jeevan. I glance up at the sky—the sun's nearly setting. We might just arrive on time.

The frown between Jeevan's eyebrows has returned and he's biting the inside of his mouth.

"Don't worry, Jeevan, it's going to be OK."

"I'm just thinking what my ma's going to say . . . or do. She might wallop me."

"She might . . . but she'll hug you after! I'm thinking the same about *my* ma."

Papa pays the driver and we get out of the rickshaw. And suddenly, there it is!

Butterflies loop through my stomach as my beautiful mountain appears before me, lit up by the blush of the setting sun.

Jeevan looks serious. "Don't worry about your parents," I say, moving closer to him. "Papa will explain."

"We were away such a long time."

"They're going to be so happy you're back . . . They'll forget all about that as soon as they see you." I twist the band that Jeevan gave me for my birthday. "And anyway, it's Divali, nobody will be angry today."

We carry on toward the mountain, passing a large handmade sign written in English and Punjabi.

ELEPHANT RIDES
HATHI CHOOTAY

A loud trumpeting echoes through the waving bamboo ahead of us and we catch up with the mahout leading his elephant into the village. He twists around in amazement. "Paras?" he asks, blinking against the dusky light. "Enakshi said she'd had your telegram—good to see you back."

"Namaste," replies Papa.

"Is that Asha with you, and Jeevan? Everyone in the village has been talking about their journey."

"Yes," says Papa proudly. "They came to find me... Just think, these two special children went so far by themselves."

We walk side by side, along the dry path toward home.

"Jeevan's ma showed everyone the postcards they sent," the mahout says, pulling the elephant's rope a little tighter. "So they've really brought you back." He smiles and looks at Jeevan and me. "How about a ride on my best elephant? Mona's all ready for the Divali celebrations."

"That's really kind," I say, "but we're in a real hurry and running will be quicker."

Papa looks toward the setting sun and laughs. "I think we have time, and if the offer's still open

I think these two deserve a hero's homecoming."

I look longingly toward Mona, draped in a shimmering gold blanket, with painted red and white dots around her eyes like a bride. She towers above me, a wide wooden seat big enough to carry us all on her back.

"Can we, Papa?"

"If you're sure?" he asks the mahout.

"Of course," he says. "You can all climb on. It will be like a proper Divali celebration, a homecoming on an elephant."

"Just like Rama and Sita," I say to Jeevan, tugging his sleeve.

"Yes," he replies shyly. "We'll be just like Rama and Sita."

The mahout calls to her softly, "Down, Mona," and she crouches low, bending her knees so we can climb up.

Papa climbs on first, lifting his foot into the stirrup against the crinkled gray skin of the elephant. Pulling on the neatly woven reins, he settles himself firmly on the seat, then holds out his hand to Jeevan, and I watch proudly as he swings him up.

"Hey, Asha," calls Jeevan, excitement dancing in his eyes, "I can see everything from here."

I'm so eager to get on I stretch toward Jeevan and slip my hand into his. He hauls me up . . . Have I gotten lighter or has he gotten stronger?

The gold thread of the elephant's blanket sparkles against the setting sun. I rearrange the silk folds of my lengha skirt so it doesn't crease, feeling every bit like a warrior queen returning to her kingdom.

With a great heave the elephant stands up, and I feel her strength under me as the mahout walks in front, leading us on the final part of our long adventure.

"I bet you never thought you'd ride home on an elephant," says Jeevan. His voice squeaks and ends in a funny deep way I've never heard before.

He looks older than when we started the journey and somehow different. There's a faint shadow of a mustache on his lip that I've only just noticed. It makes me want to run my finger along it, to check that it isn't my imagination. I want to giggle but I'm not sure why.

We climb a little hill and as we dip down the other side I see our village, *at last.* My chunni flutters behind me like the wings of a lamagaia, and it's then that I spot my nanijee circling above us. I give her a gigantic wave. My pendant rocks and she swoops down, following behind us as we get closer to the village, calling to us.

"Papa, look!"

"Asha . . . It's your nanijee, she's guiding us home," says Jeevan.

I squeeze his hand and she flies over, brushing our heads with the tips of her velvety wings. I gaze up, watching her soar into the dark pink sky with a powerful whoosh of air. "Thank you, Nanijee."

As we carry on into the village, I look down at the houses I haven't seen for so long, bundled together, keeping each other company. Higher up on the grazing plains, small shadowy dots move slowly across the mountain. *Our cows!*

People in the fields stop what they're doing and lift their heads in our direction. The air rings with the sounds of our names.

It's been nine months since Papa's seen this view. The sky is deep red, turning a darker purple as a small flock of rosefinches flit against the sky, making shapes that look like moving hearts.

The clouds shift in the breeze, puffing into different shapes. I see Lord Shiva, the warrior goddess Durga riding the tiger, the temple in the mountains, and the Holy Ganges flowing from the rock, lighting up the whole sky like a story.

Both Papa and Jeevan stare into the sky as well, but maybe I'm the only one who can see the images. It doesn't matter. I've learned to trust myself.

Mona lifts up her trunk and blows a heralding trumpet. As she quiets and continues walking, another sound drifts toward us: raised angry voices, faint at first but becoming louder.

Then I see Meena's red car parked outside our gates and I grip the reins tighter. I spot Ma in the middle of the gang but Rohan and Roopa aren't there. Why can't I see them?

"Papa, Meena's here already with her thugs," I yell. "We have to hurry. Can you stop the elephant, please?" I ask the mahout. I'm frantic now.

"Stop," says Papa, "quickly."

A crowd of villagers surround the elephant, shouting and pointing back toward our house.

"Hey," I shout at the top of my lungs. "We're back and my papa's here."

Meena stares at us. Her thugs just stand there, mouths wide open as if they've seen a ghost.

The elephant stops and kneels down and I slide off, rushing toward the crowd, followed closely by Papa and Jeevan. I see now that Rohan and Roopa are safe, standing with Jeevan's parents.

Meena steps toward us in her pristine Western clothes and dark glasses, sneering at us. Her men close in to protect her, raising their heavy wooden batons.

Ma struggles away from them, her face ashen, and runs to Papa, who pulls her to him.

"Stop," he says as the men spring forward. "There's no need for you or your men to come any farther." He delves into his pocket and brings out the compensation money and his wages and waves it in the air.

Meena looks shocked and disgusted at the same time. "Are you sure you have it all?" she says, nodding at the men to take the money.

"Wait," says Papa, and he demands to see the full details of the loan first. He reads it carefully before counting out the notes slowly. "That covers the interest too—I'll come to Sonahaar tomorrow to get the tractor back. You should be ashamed of yourselves."

Meena shrugs and flicks imaginary dirt off her sleeve. "I gave your family money when they needed it—but it was never a present."

"Get out of our village," continues Papa, his anger flaring.

Meena gestures to the men, who rush to open the car door for her. She slips inside and the darkened windows slide up soundlessly. They leave the village, the car throwing up a trail of dust and stones.

CHAPTER

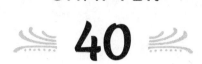

40

Early Divali fireworks spark into the dusk as the car disappears over the horizon.

"The fireworks have started!" shouts Jeevan. "And good riddance to bad rubbish."

Jeevan's parents run toward us, folding Jeevan in their arms.

"Ma," I cry, pressing my whole body into hers. "Ma, we're home."

She takes my hands, holding me away to get a proper look. "Asha! Don't ever leave like that again!" she shouts, but then pulls me to her. "I was so worried. I didn't know if I would ever see you— What have you done to your hair?"

"Don't be angry, Ma," I say. "I brought Papa home."

"Oh, Asha." Ma's tears fall onto my head. "Asha . . . You're home at last."

She wraps me in her special blue sari, embroidered with peacocks.

Papa's right behind me and hurls his arms around us all. "I wish I could stay home forever," he says. And a little bit of my happiness crumbles when I remember that he's used all his money on repaying the loan.

"Will you have to go back to Zandapur?" I whisper, just to him.

"We shouldn't think about that now," he replies.

Rohan and Roopa hold me around the waist. "We missed you," they both say.

"We didn't know if you'd come back," says Rohan.

"Your hair's gone," says Roopa.

Ma puts the marigolds she's had looped on her arm over Papa's head and buries her face into his shoulder as he holds her even closer. "What happened, Ashi? How did you find him? Your telegram said so little."

Jeevan and I share a glance and start to tell our story.

Our voices drift into the evening sky like clouds of incense. The mooing cows join in, and so do the rushing waters of the Ganges, the sweet chirruping of the rosefinches, the rhythm from my pendant, and the far-off cry of my nanijee and all the daughters from our family, raising their spirits from the past.

It's the song of the mountain and it echoes through our valley—a blessing joining us all together.

Family is the most important thing in the whole world and now that we're together again, I won't let anything separate us.

Like every Divali, there's no moon tonight, and the path leading to our house is lit with flickering deevay, just like in the paintings from the ancient texts.

We head inside as the night grows chilly, but I notice something through the back door. "Ma, Papa, look!" The well is lit up as brightly as a shrine and my nanijee is perched on the very edge of the crumbling wall. I go back outside and walk toward her.

"This is where I first saw you, wasn't it?" I close my eyes and the rhythm from my pendant buzzes through my bones, awakening the place deep in my spirit where my magical powers are born, and I move closer to the well.

Everyone gathers around, staring at my spirit bird in disbelief and admiration. Ma inches closer to her and stretches out a shaky hand.

"I think Nanijee would like it if you touched her," I say.

"M-maybe later," she says, drawing her hand back.

"It's OK, Ma." I hitch up my lengha, tucking the fabric into the waistband, and stand on the wall beside my nanijee. She walks around the edge of the well, and I'm convinced she's trying to tell me something.

"I'm going down there."

Ma jumps onto the wall too and grabs me by the arm. "Stop, Asha!"

Nanijee flies up and lands on my shoulder, flapping her wings.

"Asha knows what she's doing," cries Jeevan. "She's amazing."

I shoot him a smile. "I'm trusting myself, Ma—now you need to trust me too . . . like Nanijee does."

My nanijee jumps off my shoulder, hops toward the

opening, and peers down, pecking at the inside of the well.

"I think your spirit bird would go down with you if she could," says Jeevan. "But of course . . ."

"Her wingspan's too wide to get out," we both finish together, laughing.

"Don't be silly, Asha," says Rohan. "You can't go down there, you'll fall into the water."

I squeeze his hand. "It's OK . . . I'm used to climbing and there are footholds in the wall."

"Jeevan's right," says Papa, putting his arm around Ma. "Let her go."

"Paras!" she says, twisting her hands. "We've always told them to stay away from the well and now—oh—I can't believe you're telling her to go into it . . . Are you crazy?"

My spirit bird begins flapping her wings hysterically.

"Ma, I'm going."

"I can see that . . . but I'm staying right here." She stays close by the opening, her eyes wild with fear.

Nanijee perches next to her and makes a clucking sound.

I grip the rim and lower myself into the darkness of the well. The sides feel damp and slimy as I search for a foothold. "Shine a deeva down here," I call, my strong voice rising to the surface. There's a brick to one side of my foot and I slide onto it, trying to keep my balance.

The golden light from above flits like fireflies as it illuminates the shadows in the well, and then I spot something. A few inches below is a wide gap in the wall's surface, with a narrow ledge just below. I carefully drop down to the ledge to take a better look. I reach my hand deep inside the gap and I feel something hard. I run my fingers along its smooth edges.

"Have you found something?" calls Jeevan.

"Yes," I reply, staring up at their faces, lit by the flickering light. Butterflies dance in my stomach as I heave the object out.

It's a box wrapped in a muddied cloth. "Get ready, Papa . . . It's heavy."

I press the box, which is at least as long as my forearm, tight to my chest, hold myself firm on the bricks, and raise it as high as I can above my head, but Papa's hands are still too far away.

"I can't quite reach it, Asha, and there's not enough room to climb in."

"Papa, it's really heavy," I pant, my legs trembling. "I . . . I can't hold it for much longer."

"I'll grab your legs," says Jeevan's papa to mine, "so you can lean in farther."

"Someone's going to get hurt," cries Ma. "Just get Asha out."

"Here, Papa." I stretch as much as I can, pushing hard against the wet walls.

Papa's hands grasp the box and he hoists it up out of the depths of the well. I let out a hot breath of relief.

"Come up quickly so we can see what it is," says Jeevan, his face full of excitement.

My nanijee is still there waiting for me, drawing me to her with wings unfolded like the god Garuda. "I'm coming," I call.

"Grab hold," says Papa, reaching farther down until his hands grasp mine firmly.

Legs shaking, I push myself out of the dank darkness into the halo of happy faces.

Everyone circles me as I tear off the dirty cloth to

reveal a box made from smooth shisham wood. The spirit bird ruffles her feathers, hops closer, and taps the ornate catch with her beak.

"Look how she's helping," squeals Roopa, stroking her wing.

I lift the lid to reveal layers of dusty gold jewelry, bridal headdresses, ornate bangles, all laid neatly, filling the box to the top. "I can't believe it," I gasp, cradling it against my chest so everyone can see the jewels lit up against the deevay.

I feel a rhythm so powerful that it transports me to another world and I see the beautiful face of my nanijee and all the forgotten daughters of my family calling to me from the distant past, sending their blessings. I see the story of each piece of gold, how it was given with love at a special time, and it touches my heart.

"It's all the daughters' gold . . . You found it!" cries Ma, astounded.

My heart clatters against my chest. The story was true!

Ma stretches out her hand, and this time she lightly

touches my spirit bird's golden feathers. "M-Ma?" she whispers, wiping her cheek.

"Maybe we can buy a new tractor now and keep the farm going," I say. "And Papa won't have to go back to the city—and we won't ever have to leave for England."

"Your ma can make her famous mango chutney," says Jeevan, his mind whizzing with ideas. "Your uncle Neel can help export it."

"Great idea," I reply.

"Maybe we can set up mountain lodges for tourists," he continues, getting more excited.

"And you can give night tours and explain the stars." I smile.

Everyone carries on chattering, discussing new projects, laughing, and joking. I walk toward the shisham tree with my nanijee following behind and sit on the cool damp ground. I clasp my nanijee gently in my arms and she moves toward me, our foreheads touching. We stay like this, staring deep into each other's eyes, previous lives flashing before us, comforted by the power of eternal reincarnation.

After one final embrace she turns her head to the

amazed faces watching us, raises her immense wings, and flies into the ink-black sky.

"Don't go too far."

I know now that if you believe in yourself, you can do anything for the people you love.

I run over to Jeevan, slip my hand in his.

"Friends forever?" he says, turning to face me.

"Friends forever," I say. "Whatever the future holds."

LETTER FROM THE AUTHOR

I was born in northern Punjab on a farm close to the Himalayas. My grandfather died when my dad was only twelve and so it was left to my grandmother, my majee, to look after five children and keep the farm going with help from my great-uncle. As a woman this would have been a challenging and difficult task, especially since my family had a high position in the village and as such she would have been closely observed.

Amongst the other animals on the farm, we had a camel and a wild monkey, Oma, who became part of the family. At nightfall, the skies were alight with millions of stars and this is when we used to set up a fire outside, make toffee popcorn, and tell stories. When I returned to India for the first time, I was amazed at how well-preserved the farm was. It was so beautiful: You could see wide views of bright green fields of sugarcane from the first-floor balconies. When we made a cup of tea, guess where the milk came from? Directly from the cow into the cup!

My lovely uncle Lashkar was the first member of the family to move to the UK and, once he had settled, he wanted all his brothers to join him. So like many families at that time, when I was a year and a half, we moved to the UK too. My great-uncle stayed behind to look after the farm.

Imagine how it must have felt to leave everything behind and go to a place practically halfway round the world! But we were a very close-knit family and my earliest memories are of big gatherings where my uncles would keep all the memories of the farm alive by telling funny stories. One of the favorite stories was how Oma used to love taking my brother off to the neem tree in the farmyard, where she would rock him to sleep in her arms.

The story my majee always told was of me standing on the wall of the well, which was dangerously deep, bawling my eyes out as the monsoon rain lashed down, and how she ran to my rescue.

There was always lots of laughter on these occasions and my mum would cook up amazing food for everyone. One of her specialties was spiced potato parathay, a sort of whole wheat flatbread layered with butter and cooked on a tava until puffed and crispy.

I wrote *Asha and the Spirit Bird* as the dissertation element of my MA in Creative Writing, and when I was thinking of ideas, I just knew that the heart of my story would take me back to the land of my birth and back to my majee.

The seed of the story began with an image of a little girl on a farm in India, playing in the dirt with water that she had collected from the well.

I couldn't shake this image away, so I began to take my own memories, twisting them into a magical story. I asked myself lots of what-if questions . . . What if we had stayed on the farm? What if things got tough and my dad had to go off to the city to work? What if we had to borrow money to make ends meet and we couldn't pay it back?

And what if our ancestors stay with us in spirit to help in times of need?

Jasbinder Bilan

ACKNOWLEDGMENTS

My first thanks go to my huge and loving family, who have waved the victory flags for me all along the way, from the moment I picked up my pen to the wonderful moment of seeing it in print. In age order: Balraj, Sherry, Randhiraj, Dip, and Amolack, and of course to my lovely mum, Gurjinder, and my dad, who made the best milk kulfi! To my uncle Gael, who cried when I was the first to go to university, and to my cousins Mindy, Michael, and Sunny. To my uncle Lashkar and aunt Paramjeet for the happy memories of countryside adventures with lashings of cake and tea.

Heartfelt thanks to my husband, Ian, for his

patience throughout and for not allowing me to starve while I spent long hours writing, and also to my sons, Gem and Satchen, for continuously asking how it was all going.

The seed for *Asha and the Spirit Bird* was first sown when I bravely quit my teaching job and enrolled in the amazing MA Creative Writing for Young People course at Bath Spa University. Thank you to my tutors: Julia Green for being there from the start, Steve Voake for his positivity and suggestion for a *kapow* opening, and Lucy Christopher for showing me the magic of pushing your setting as far as it will let you. To Janine Amos and John McLay for sharing their extensive knowledge of the publishing world. Thank you to Barry Cunningham, Kesia Lupo, and the panel of judges for choosing my story to win the 2017 *Times*/Chicken House prize over all the other amazing ones—you made my dream come true! To all the team at Chicken House, especially Kesia for being such an insightful editor. To Dion Mehaga Bangun Djayasaputra for creating the most beautiful cover. It gave me tingly goose bumps when I first saw the way he imagined my spirit bird. Huge thanks also to Elizabeth Parisi. To Sam Palazzi for loving my story and taking it across the ocean to sing its praises, and to the Scholastic team for welcoming it with open arms. Thanks also to Jazz Bartlett, Laura Myers, and Elinor Bagenal.

To the wonderful Ben, my agent, for his enthusiasm and expert eye, and for finding me glittering sea gifts.

To my friend Judy, who I know would have adored my story and is always with me in spirit.

A massive thank-you to Miranda and Mel, who really are the dream team. You were there from the very beginning. You told it how it was, gave me just what I needed when I needed it . . . tissues, tea, champagne. I couldn't have done this without you.

To fellow writers at Bath Spa MAWYP: Sarah, Carlyn, Wendy, Jennifer, Charlotte, and Tracy for continuing to drink tea and eat cake at every opportunity. To Cal Sharp for all her technical wizardry in helping me navigate the world of websites.

Thank you to dear Rachael and my young readers Bel and Mintie for loving Asha's story without reservation.

To the amazing staff at my primary school, Mellers in Nottingham, especially Mr. Stanton and Mr. Ferrigan, who packed fun, songs, and laughter into their schoolbags every day, and to Mrs. Wallis, who let me be creative and who taught me to never give up.

To the brave huntress Sarah Driver, author extraordinaire, for all her encouragement and for her endorsement.

Finally, a huge thank-you to my readers. I hope you've enjoyed this book—without you, would it simply be a story gathering dust? The magic happens once the cover is opened and you decide to enter.